'Did you forget your key?'

Dr Patrick Delan shook his head. 'When I said I lived here, I didn't mean in Florence's apartment. I live on the top floor.'

Rebecca felt her spirits rise again. How silly of her to jump to conclusions. Not that it was any business of hers what these two got up to!

Margaret Barker pursued a variety of interesting careers before she became a full-time author. Besides holding a BA degree in French and linguistics, she is a licentiate of the Royal Academy of Music, a state registered nurse and a qualified teacher. Happily married, she has two sons, a daughter and an increasing number of grandchildren. She lives with her husband in a sixteenth-century thatched house near the sea.

Previous Titles

ALL FOR LOVE
TROPICAL PARADISE

FOR LOVE'S SAKE ONLY

BY

MARGARET BARKER

MILLS & BOON LIMITED
ETON HOUSE   18–24 PARADISE ROAD
RICHMOND   SURREY   TW9 1SR

First published in Great Britain 1992
by Mills & Boon Limited

© Margaret Barker 1992

Australian copyright 1992
Philippine copyright 1992
This edition 1992

ISBN 0 263 77630 1

Set in 10 on 12 pt Linotron Times
03-9204-49474
Typeset in Great Britain by Centracet, Cambridge
Made and printed in Great Britain

CHAPTER ONE

REBECCA jumped hurriedly to the other side of the pavement as the early morning cleansing lorry swished a torrent of water over the rue Ste-Catherine.

'*Bonjour, mademoiselle. Ça va?*'

Rebecca smiled back at the cheery young driver, high and dry in his cab, as she shook the spray from her travel-worn shoes. She was past caring about her appearance after the long overnight coach journey from London. Curled up in the cramped seat for what had seemed like an eternity, she'd somehow managed to accumulate more creases in her supposedly crease-resistant catsuit than the label had predicted.

Deciding to try out her rusty French, she called back, '*Bonjour, monsieur. Oui, ça va bien, merci.*'

Not strictly true! Everything was far from OK, but Rebecca had found that if she put on a brave face things usually changed for the better.

'*Ah, vous êtes anglaise, mademoiselle.* Good morning!'

Was it so obvious that she wasn't Parisian? She supposed it probably was extremely evident, as her eye caught sight of a chic French lady stepping suddenly from behind long billowing curtains on to a first-floor balcony that overlooked the street. Everything about the woman spelt luxury, privilege, leisure, Parisian elegance.

5

The cleansing lorry had trundled on down the street, and Rebecca paused for a moment to watch the woman. She saw the obviously well-manicured scarlet nails take hold of the wrought-iron balustrade. In her ivory silk négligé the woman looked the essence of chic, and Rebecca couldn't help but feel a pang of envy. She could almost smell the expensive French perfume wafting down to mingle with the disinfected aroma of the newly washed street.

The woman raised her hand to her mouth and blew a kiss to someone in a midnight-blue Peugeot down in the street below. Rebecca could see that a couple of children were waving madly through the back windscreen and a man was starting up the engine. Intrigued, she moved hurriedly along so that she could get a glimpse of the man who belonged to the vision on the balcony.

Mm, he was nice. . .in fact, he was more than nice. He was absolutely dishy!

Rebecca stifled a sigh as the man turned his head before moving out into the traffic. His light brown, beautifully cut hair had a distinctly gold tinge and she was sure his eyes would be a piercing blue, but she couldn't make them out from this distance.

Sister Rebecca Manson, she told herself severely, as the car swept past her, you shouldn't be having such adolescent fantasies! You're a fully-fledged engaged lady with a loving fiancé who depends on your continued support. In fact, she knew Chris would be devastated if he thought she was even glancing admiringly at another man. It wouldn't help his medical recovery at all to know that occasionally she felt a bit hemmed in by the events of the past year.

Good old Rebecca. . .she'll cope, everybody always said. So she always had done. But just sometimes— like now, at the end of a wearying journey, by the cheapest possible form of transport—she'd like to be pampered. Pampered like the woman on the balcony. She looked back, but the woman had disappeared inside. Probably to sip coffee before she took the poodle for a stroll.

Now you're being bitchy! she told herself. But the woman had all the characteristics Rebecca wished she had. Long legs that would make her much taller than Rebecca's five feet two inches, short, well-cut dark hair that looked as if it had been styled by an artist, the exact opposite of Rebecca's long, unruly carrot-col-oured hair. She thought it was funny how in novels women were described as having beautiful golden hair, but no one had ever referred to her hair as anything other than carrot or red. Even Chris still insisted on calling her Carrot-top, just as he'd done all those years ago at school.

Better get a move on, she thought, quickening her pace. It's going to take a miracle to get my act together before I meet the Medical Director at ten o'clock.

She only hoped there would be a shower available before her interview. The arrangements for somewhere to stay during her twelve-month contract had been rather vague. She had gathered that there was no nurses' home in the exclusive Clinique Ste-Catherine. When she had telephoned from England, a rather impatient receptionist had informed her in rapid

French that most of the staff had their own apartments near to the Clinique.

Rebecca glanced upwards at the apartment block she was now passing. It looked a very pricy area! She doubted very much if she could afford to live here. Maybe a long journey out to the suburbs would have to be made.

She changed hands on her suitcase, but it felt just as heavy. She wondered how much longer it would be before she reached the Clinique. And then, as she turned the corner, she saw a discreet sign pointing along a side road.

'Clinique Ste-Catherine,' she read.

This was it! This was where she would work for the next year. . .provided that she was still acceptable after the initial three months' trial. And provided Chris didn't throw a wobbly and demand she return home to look after him during his convalescence.

The clinic was set back from the road, approached by wide, sweeping steps which led to a revolving glass door. It was difficult enough to get into a section of the door with her suitcase upended, but it was almost impossible to get out of the contraption when she revolved to the inside.

She'd planned to make an entrance, but found herself being literally spilled on to the marble floor. The catch on her ancient suitcase that had already groaned and protested at the rough treatment it had received at the hands of the coach driver now sprang open, to disgorge the entire contents at the feet of an unsuspecting man.

Rebecca fell to her knees and started grappling with

the case, stuffing everything out of sight. Back in England she'd packed in a hurry, and some of her garments left a lot to be desired. She now regretted her decision to bring some of her old tried and testeds with the idea of having a shopping spree when she got the feel of the place.

She gave a mental groan as she pushed her old jeans out of sight. Her eyes travelled to the man's trouser-clad legs and she raised her head to see what he looked like. She was used to craning her neck to people, but this was ridiculous!

One glance at the man's face told her that it was the heart-throb she'd seen driving away only minutes before. As if to confirm her suspicions, her ears now tuned in to the sound of children's voices. A small boy and girl were seated on either side of the receptionist, doodling happily on large sheets of typing paper.

Rebecca's mind registered relief as she realised that she was able to understand the receptionist's French. The woman was telling Mr Heart-throb not to worry, she would take care of the children until it was time for school. And from the deferential tone of her voice it was obvious that he was somebody important.

Everything had seemed to happen as if in slow motion. Rebecca felt as if she were taking part in a film. It had been a crazy, nightmarish comedy until this moment. But now the man was looking down at her with concern in his eyes. . .and yes, they were a piercing blue colour, just as she'd hoped they would be. . .and, unbelievably, he was holding out his hand and asking if he could help her.

Rebecca drew in a deep breath as she took hold of

his hand. When she rose to her full height she realised that her knees were shaking. Well, what could she expect after a night without sleep? But she knew it wasn't the lack of sleep. It was the effect this charismatic man was having on her.

She stared up into the blue eyes as she cleared her throat and launched into her well-prepared speech, introducing herself in French and saying she had an appointment at ten o'clock with Dr Patrick Delan and was there anywhere she could go to clean up first? She'd come to Paris on the overnight coach from London and——

'Have you had breakfast?' the man broke into her nervous verbal torrent.

She shook her head. 'I really should——'

He stretched out his hand. 'I'm Patrick Delan. Come and have breakfast with me. I'm glad you're early, because I've got a busy schedule this morning.'

Rebecca realised he was speaking perfect English with only a hint of an accent. He switched to French as he spoke to his receptionist.

'We'll be in the Café Mozart, Jacqueline. See if you can fix this case for Sister Manson. And you children, behave yourselves at school today. Maman will pick you up at lunchtime. . .'

As if in a dream, she realised that they were halfway out through the revolving doors. Dr Delan's arm had propelled her in the right direction, and she now stood on the top step trying to make sense of the last few minutes. Glancing down at her dishevelled catsuit, she felt like a fish out of water beside the sophisticated, handsome French doctor in his dove-grey designer suit.

'It will be impossible to park, so we'll walk down to the café. You're not too tired, I hope?'

She assured him that she felt fine. His concern was so touching! It was just what she needed. She began to feel refreshed already. The need for a shower receded as she strode out beside the tall, invigorating doctor, her short legs taking two strides to every one of his.

They were passing the apartment block where the woman in his life had waved farewell. She glanced up at his face, but he didn't react in any way. Why were they going to a café when he could have taken her in home? Or maybe it wasn't his home. Maybe this was just his mistress, the mother of his children. Now there was an intriguing thought! Perhaps she'd been reading too many romantic novels.

Rebecca smiled to herself. She'd always loved to weave stories around people she met. Sometimes she wasn't far wrong, but in many cases she was way off course. One thing was for sure in this situation. The dishy doctor was spoken for. . .and so was she!

The journey to the bottom of the street was accomplished in half the time it had taken her to walk up there weighed down by her heavy suitcase. Not only was she now relieved of her impedimenta, but her legs seemed to have taken on a new lightness of step. She was walking on air and feeling ten feet tall. . .well, not quite! She still had to crane her neck to look up at her exciting companion.

His arm guided her through the door of the Café Mozart and on towards a corner table. There was a delicious smell of coffee beans and fresh-baked croissants. A waiter came over to their table, greeting the doctor effusively as he spread a new cloth on the table.

The coffee tasted as delicious as it smelt. Rebecca's spirits had risen sky-high in the preceding few minutes. She turned to look at the man who was to be her boss and saw that he was already scrutinising her carefully. To her annoyance a deep blush spread over her face. She could feel it diffusing over her cheeks and knew that the freckles on either side of her nose would look as if they were joined together.

'Where did you learn to speak such good English?' she asked hurriedly, in an effort to cover up her embarrassment.

Dr Delan smiled and leaned back in his chair. 'My mother was English. She made a point of packing me off to my grandmother's house in Devon every summer. After a few weeks with my English cousins I could chatter away quite happily.'

Rebecca stared at him. 'What a coincidence! The same thing used to happen to me. I used to be sent to my French grandmother when I was very small. But she died when I was eight; my parents split up soon afterwards and there were no more visits to France—which is one reason why my French isn't as good as your English.'

'It will improve with practice. But many of our patients are English—that was why I wanted to take on an English nursing sister. The London agency who recommended you told me that your fiancé would be travelling to Paris with you,' he added.

Rebecca took a deep breath. The memory of Chris's accident was still painful for her.

'Christopher Preston, my fiancé, has had an unfortunate accident. He was rock-climbing six weeks ago and he fell, fracturing his left femur. He was to have taken up a post in a language school here. But now, of course, he's had to give up his contract.'

The doctor's eyes flickered with genuine concern. 'I'm sorry to hear that. Which part of the femur did he fracture?'

'The mid-shaft. He's still in hospital on traction. It looked as if I might have to cancel my appointment too, but we agreed that I shouldn't change my plans.'

Rebecca took a sip of her strong coffee as she thought that wasn't strictly true. Chris had sulked for several days when she'd pointed out that one of them had to work if they were to save enough to get married. And the Paris job was the best salary she'd ever had. . .almost double what she'd been making at St Celine's in London. And the chance of working with the great Patrick Delan wasn't to be turned down lightly. She'd been very lucky to land this appointment, and, besides, she was under no illusions about the necessity of continuing her career after marriage. So, the more experience she got, the better it would be for them.

'You look—how do you say?—miles away,' he said quietly.

She smiled. 'I'm sorry, I was thinking about how much easier it would have been to stay in England.'

'I'm glad you didn't.'

She swallowed hard as she heard the concerned tone of his voice. 'But you haven't asked me any questions about my nursing credentials. I thought you were going to. . .'

'I know all I need to from reading your curriculum vitae. From a qualifications and experience point of view I can't fault you. And from what I've seen so far I think you'll fit in perfectly.'

She smiled. 'Even though I threw my belongings all over your reception area?'

He laughed, a deep rich sound that seemed to indicate to Rebecca an inbuilt *joie de vivre* that would be difficult to shatter. 'The children will enjoy helping to mend the suitcase. You'll probably find it covered in Sellotape when you get back.'

She hesitated. 'How old are your children?'

'Oliver is eight and Louise is seven. . .but they're not my children. They belong to a very close friend of mine.'

Very close! Rebecca thought, and wondered what the children's father thought of the arrangement.

'Their father was my colleague before he died,' he added.

It was uncanny. . .almost as if he'd been reading her mind! She glanced up at his face and saw a look of deep pain in the expressive blue eyes.

'You must be a great help to your colleague's widow,' she commented gently. In her mind's eye she could see the attractive woman on the balcony. But now she was able to view her with dispassion. A young woman left alone with two small children was not to be envied.

The doctor gave a deep sigh. 'I do what I can. It's the least I can do in the circumstances.'

Rebecca waited for him to elucidate. It was the strangest feeling, but here she was listening to the confidences of her boss on their first meeting together. Already she could feel a rapport between them. . .and she felt that Dr Delan had noticed it too.

He looked uncharacteristically sad. 'Four years ago my wife, Sophie, and I were invited to a dinner party at the house of a colleague across the other side of Paris. We had arranged to take Florence and Michel with us in our car. At the last moment there was an emergency at the Clinique. I had to deal with it, so my wife went to the party alone with our friends. Driving home afterwards, Sophie crashed the car, killing herself and Florence's husband Michel.'

The everyday sounds in the café seemed too loud. Rebecca wanted to silence the noise so that she could say soothing words that would ease away the obvious suffering of her companion.

'I'm so very sorry,' she said softly, realising how banal and inadequate were her sentiments.

'Four years is a long time,' he replied, a strange faraway look in his eyes. 'Time is a great healer. But the guilt is always with me.'

'Guilt?' she queried.

He nodded sadly. 'It was my wife who took away the life of Florence's husband. Sophie had drunk too much at the party. She should never have been behind the wheel of the car. If I'd been with her I would never have allowed it.'

'And so you go on torturing yourself with remorse about what might have been,' whispered Rebecca, almost to herself.

She saw the puzzled look in his eyes and knew, with relief, that he hadn't heard what she'd said. She couldn't understand how she had dared to be so bold with this man whom she'd only just met.

'We all have our crosses to bear,' he said softly.

'Yes, we do,' she breathed, realising with a surge of irrepressible emotion that the two of them had a great deal in common.

She became aware that their waiter was hurrying across the room, threading his way purposefully between the crowded tables. He bent his head and spoke urgently to Dr Delan, who nodded and rose immediately to his feet.

'I have to return at once to the Clinique,' he told her. 'You can stay and finish your coffee if you like.'

'I'd like to come with you.'

As she stood up she saw the approving look on his face.

'Would you like to assist me this morning?' he asked. 'You're not too tired?'

She shook her head. 'I feel fine.'

And, amazingly, she realised it was true.

CHAPTER TWO

REBECCA was relieved to find there was time to take a shower before starting work. As the refreshing torrent cascaded over her skin she reviewed the situation she'd landed herself in. There was no doubt about it, Dr Patrick Delan was a dream! The sort of man who, had she been free, would have sent her into a complete spin. . .well, she had to admit she wasn't exactly in control of herself at the moment!

She turned off the water and stepped out of the cubicle, wrapping herself in a large fluffy white towel. Mm, the luxury of the Clinique Ste-Catherine was beginning to get through to her. Now she simply had to concentrate on the task in hand and forget her attraction towards Patrick Delan. The whole idea was preposterous. She was going to work alongside him now as if he were nothing more than a piece of highly specialised medical equipment!

She cast her eyes appraisingly around the room in which Jacqueline, the receptionist, had installed her. Jacqueline had explained that it was a private room used only when all the other rooms were full.

A white uniform sister's dress had been laid out on the bed. Rebecca remembered having to send her measurements after she'd been appointed and, with relief, she noted that the dress looked small enough for her. It was obviously brand new, tailored to her requirements. The Clinique seemed to spare no expense.

Her battered suitcase lay open beside the dress. It looked as if someone had unsuccessfully attempted to mend the lock. She decided there and then to buy a new case with her first pay cheque. It would have to wait until the end of the month.

She extricated her navy blue hospital belt from the depths of the case and ran her fingers over the silver buckle, thinking how proud she had been when she had successfully completed her training at St Celine's. And Chris had been there in the front row of the lecture theatre, clapping and applauding as Matron presented her with the prize for surgery.

In fact, now she came to think of it, Chris had always been there. First it was in the primary school when he had defended her against an older bully boy who had tried to pinch her biscuits at playtime. And later on, when they both went off to the co-ed comprehensive school, he had supported everything she did. They'd been like brother and sister for as long as she could remember.

She frowned as she deliberately tried to push aside the memories. She couldn't remember when her feelings for Chris had changed from being sisterly, but they had. . .hadn't they? It was true she didn't experience shivers of excitement whenever he came near, as she had been led to believe in certain novels she'd read, but then Chris was different. . .he was simply Chris. Good, solid, dependable. . .deeply boring at times and full of his own importance, but. . .

There was a quiet tapping on the door. Hurriedly

she fastened the belt around her dress and went to open it.

A young nurse told her that Dr Delan was waiting for her and she would take her to him. Closing the door behind her, Rebecca followed the girl down a long, white-carpeted corridor.

White carpet! she registered. How do they keep it so clean and spotless? There must be an army of domestics.

The girl ushered her into a private room and then quietly went away. Rebecca could see Patrick Delan pacing the floor by the window. He moved towards her and stood towering above her, his handsome face creased into a frown.

She tried to ignore the *frisson* of sensation that ran through her.

'I was led to believe that my patient was well advanced in labour,' Patrick Delan began. 'Now it appears that it may be a false alarm. Her husband has just telephoned to say they will be delayed. But a promise is a promise. I gave my word to my patient that I would deliver her baby, so I must make myself available. Come and sit over here by the window while we wait.'

They sat on either side of the long casement windows that looked out over the busy street below.

He leaned towards Rebecca. 'At least it will give me time to fill you in on our patient. Her name is Jane Gordon; she's English. Her husband is a sales director for an Anglo-French firm dealing in computers, I believe. Anyway, they've been living in Paris for a couple of years. I don't foresee any problems—she's had a normal pregnancy, and has taken care of herself. But we must be aware of the fact that she's forty-two and this is her first pregnancy.'

Rebecca nodded. 'This seems to be happening more and more these days. Women are leaving childbearing until they've established a career.'

He nodded in agreement. 'Exactly. You have the same syndrome in London, then?'

'Oh, yes. I've delivered several healthy babies to patients who would have been regarded as too old only a generation ago. These women seem to make excellent mothers, because the babies are so definitely wanted.'

He smiled. 'I'm glad you have this attitude. I can see you're going to be an asset to the clinic. And the fact that you're English will endear you to the English clientele. There is quite a large English community here in Paris now.'

She smiled back at him, feeling her confidence grow.

'There's just one thing,' he added. 'I hadn't realised that you were so—how shall I put it?—petite. How is your general health? I mean, are you strong enough to withstand the busy life we have here at the clinic?'

Rebecca took a deep breath. 'Dr Delan, you're not the first person to doubt my strength, but, I assure you, I may be small, but I'm very tough. I mean, I've just travelled overnight from England on the bus, getting very little sleep and——'

'But I had no idea. I assumed you'd flown over. Why didn't you take the plane or——?'

'I took the cheapest form of transport,' she declared bluntly. 'But as I was saying, I'm fighting fit and——'

'You must rest, Sister Manson. I don't want——'

The door burst open and a stretcher was pushed into the room. The woman lying on it was crying softly, holding tightly to the hand of her husband, who looked absolutely terrified.

The patient stretched out a hand towards the doctor. 'Oh, Dr Delan, thank goodness you're here! I'm sure it's a false alarm, but I've got such terrible back-ache. Brian has been rubbing my back, but it's not doing any good.'

'Mr Gordon, why don't you go downstairs and have a cup of coffee? I'll call you when things start moving,' Patrick Delan said quietly.

The husband's face registered relief as he kissed his wife and beat a hasty retreat.

'Jane, this is Sister Manson—and yes, she's as English as you are.'

The patient gave a wan smile. 'Lovely! I don't think my French is good enough to describe how I'm feeling at the moment. Have you had any babies, Sister? No, I don't suppose you have, you look far too young.'

Rebecca smiled and took hold of her patient's hand. 'I'm twenty-five, old enough, but I haven't got around to it yet.'

'Well, don't leave it as long as I did. I'm old enough to be your mother, and I feel dreadful.'

'Now let me help you on to the bed so that we can examine you,' Rebecca said gently.

'Further on than we thought,' Patrick Delan announced after his examination. 'Your cervix is well dilated, Jane, so you're almost ready for the second stage of labour. Do you remember what you learned at the ante-natal classes?'

The patient screwed up her face as another contraction began. 'I don't remember anything at the moment,' she replied in a voice that threatened to dissolve into panic.

Rebecca took hold of her hand and squeezed tightly. 'Breathe with me, Jane.'

The panic in Jane's eyes began to evaporate as she concentrated on the breathing.

'If you like, you can have some inhalation analgesia,' Dr Delan put in gently. 'You remember we discussed it only last week. I know you were against it then, but if——'

'No, thanks. I want to experience all of it,' the mother-to-be declared. 'I haven't waited nine months to be pipped at the post.'

The doctor smiled. 'That's my girl. Now, we're going to take you down to the delivery-room, so it's back on to the trolley.'

The porter, who had been asked to wait outside, was now summoned back into the room. Rebecca noticed a new calmness had descended on her patient. Everything was going like clockwork now. She prayed there would be no last-minute complications. She was keeping a constant check on the foetal heartbeat and the mother's blood-pressure—all perfectly normal, but, as Dr Delan had told her, they must constantly remind themselves that this was a mother who was past the usual age of giving birth.

It seemed only minutes before delivery of the baby was imminent. Two nurses had joined them in the delivery suite. Rebecca and the doctor had put on sterile gowns and gloves and the patient was fully prepared. She had chosen to be delivered in the conventional way, lying semi-recumbent with her knees flexed.

During a break in contractions, Jane had told Rebecca that she'd considered all the new ideas about birthing positions and had discarded them.

'Somehow I couldn't see myself thrashing around in a swimming-pool or sitting on a birthing stool,' she'd told Rebecca. 'I'm too old.'

Rebecca had given her patient an encouraging smile, wiped down her face gently with a soft sponge and told her that she was a model patient.

'One of the best patients I've delivered,' Rebecca declared. 'Maturity can be a great asset.'

And now they had reached the final stage, and the atmosphere in the delivery-room was charged with excitement. Rebecca never ceased to feel thrilled when a new life was about to appear. The head was emerging, and Dr Delan took hold of it, keeping it flexed to control its exit and prevent damage to the perineum.

'Pant with me now, Jane,' Rebecca said.

Her patient clung to her hand as she panted. Rebecca could see that the remainder of the head and face had been born slowly and safely. Dr Delan was feeling for the umbilical cord by sliding a finger under the pubic arch. With an expert movement of his finger he slipped it over the baby's head out of harm's way. The next contraction delivered the shoulders and body, and the doctor placed the new baby on to the mother's abdomen.

'It's a boy,' he told the new mother.

'Let me hold him. . .oh, he's wonderful!' Jane Gordon was crying with happiness.

Rebecca looked across the table at Dr Delan. There was a gentle look of relief in his eyes. Everything had gone according to plan, but the feeling of relief was always there at the end of a delivery. However you put on a brave face for the patient there was always a nagging fear of failure at the back of your mind. You could never afford to relax, and they had both known this—especially in view of the patient's age.

'Thank you, Sister,' Dr Delan said quietly. 'And now I really think you should go off duty and have that rest I prescribed some time ago. My nurses will assist me with the final stage.'

Rebecca knew she must take his advice. She'd been running on increased adrenalin for the past couple of hours, and suddenly she felt deflated. And she didn't want anyone to think she wasn't strong enough.

As she left the delivery suite, her legs started to weaken with each step. She shouldn't have insisted on working. . .but she was glad she had done. It had been a good opportunity to get to know her boss. They'd both been sizing each other up during the delivery, and she felt they would make a good team.

Back in the room that Jacqueline had assigned to her, she crawled on to the bed, loosening her belt but feeling too weary to undress. She closed her eyes, planning to rest for a few minutes until she felt strong enough to take off her clothes and get under the covers.

The shrilling of the bedside phone awoke her. In a state of complete disorientation she put out her hand and clutched at the handset.

'*Mademoiselle, c'est Jacqueline ici.*'

Rebecca was instantly awake and trying to grapple with the receptionist's torrent of French. It appeared that Dr Delan wanted her to join him for dinner at the home of his friend Madame Florence Maurin.

Dinner? Rebecca glanced at her watch and realised that she must have slept through the day. Running a hand through her long, tousled red hair, she told the receptionist she would be happy to join Dr Delan and Madame Maurin.

'Dr Delan would like you to meet him downstairs in half an hour, *mademoiselle*, so he can show you the way to Madame Maurin's apartment.'

She assured the receptionist that she would be there. As she put down the phone her mind switched into top gear. How to transform herself in thirty minutes from a sleepy-eyed, tangle-haired girl into someone who could hold her own against the chic Parisian widow?

But it's not a contest, she reminded herself forcefully, as she made for the shower, clutching shampoo and conditioner. Her hair would never dry in time. . .there was so much of it! Perhaps she should have it cut while she was out here in Paris. Maybe it would make her look more elegant.

She caught a glimpse of herself in the misted-up mirror as she stepped out of the shower and thought, No chance! No one would ever describe her as elegant.

Oh, well, she would just have to develop her own style. She ran over to examine the contents of her suitcase, now deposited on the white-carpeted floor, near the window. She pulled out her old dressing-gown and wrapped herself in it. How long had she been hanging on to this old thing?. . .since PTS? No, longer! She'd had it when she was still at school!

She glanced out through the billowing net curtains. The September sky was still blue, but the sun had disappeared somewhere over the Bois de Boulogne at the top of the rue Ste-Catherine. It was the in-between season, when you couldn't wear summer cotton and you hadn't got any new autumn things. . .well, she hadn't, anyway!

Her suit. . .that was the thing to wear. Black was chic—and safe! She could dress it up with her grand-mother's pearls, the only item of real jewellery she possessed. The high-heeled black shoes from Roland Cartier gave her new confidence as the inches increased. She swept back her half-dry hair and piled it on top of her head, securing it with a huge golden clasp.

The bedside phone rang.

Dr Delan was waiting, Jacqueline informed her, in a crisp, no-nonsense voice.

'I'm coming, I'm on my way.'

Her voice sounded breathless, excited, full of anticipation.

Calm down! she told herself. You're going to meet your boss's girlfriend. Hardly an event to warrant such panic!

He was waiting for her down in the lobby. He came towards her, and her knees felt as if they were turning to jelly. She took his outstretched hand and felt the warm clasp of friendship.

'I didn't mean to rush you, Rebecca, but Florence is

a stickler for punctuality. She prides herself on her cooking and hates her guests to be late.'

His eyes were twinkling with amusement, but Rebecca's feeling of nervousness returned. It had temporarily disappeared at the sight of Patrick Delan's warm expression, but now she remembered that she must stop fantasising about this attractive man. She mustn't aggravate her hostess, that unknown woman who seemed to hold all the trump cards in her elegant hand.

'I'm sorry to delay you,' Rebecca apologised. 'I slept all through the day.'

'I'm glad you did. You must have been exhausted after your tiring journey.'

He tucked his hand under her arm and steered her towards the revolving door.

Outside, the warm September air was cooling down at the end of the day. Rebecca caught a whiff of the delicious smell of freshly baked bread from the *boulangerie* along the road. People were hurrying out of its door carrying their evening baguettes home for the family dinner that would signal the end of the working day and the beginning of the evening's relaxation. There was a feeling of anticipation in the air. Everyone looked happy and full of hope. As she stepped down from the stone steps, Rebecca thought that there was no doubt about it, the people of Paris seemed to know what they wanted from life—a good home, a loving family and enough money to make life comfortable.

She fell into step with Dr Delan, or rather into steps, because she took two to each one of his. She'd rather hoped they would go in his blue Peugeot, but realised that the evening traffic was impossible to negotiate in the narrow streets, made even narrower by the parking and sometimes double parking of the cars on both sides. But it was good to step out beside her handsome boss, revelling in the admiring glances and deferential greetings of the passers-by.

They stopped in front of the tall, cream-coloured stone apartment building she had passed earlier in the day. The huge plate glass door was firmly shut. Patrick Delan pressed several numbers on the code selector at the side of the door.

'All the occupants and their close friends know the code of the month,' he explained. 'But sometimes the code has to be changed more frequently if too many outsiders have been given access to it.'

The door swung open and they went into a wide lobby, flanked by a miniature indoor garden, illuminated by hidden spotlights. Rebecca's high heels sank noiselessly into the deep pile of the carpet as they moved towards the reception area.

A thick-set, middle-aged, balding concierge came hurrying out of his glass-fronted cubicle, one hand outstretched in welcome and the other struggling to pull a jacket over his obviously unsuitable sleeveless vest.

'*Monsieur le docteur, madame vous attend en haut. Elle m'a teléphoné pour——*'

'*Merci, Pierre.*' Patrick Delan assured the concierge that they wouldn't keep Madame Maurin waiting any longer.

Pierre ushered them into the lift and they were taken swiftly and silently to the first floor.

'Hardly worth the effort,' Patrick Delan said as they stepped out and the doors of the lift closed. 'But our concierge likes to be helpful. When he's not around, I bound up the stairs and get here in half the time.'

'I suppose you have to make frequent visits,' Rebecca began, and saw the flickering of a smile on the doctor's handsome face.

'I live here,' he told her.

She felt her heart sink. She knew that anatomically this was impossible. She'd read about it in love stories where the heroine thought she was going to lose the hero, and she'd always scoffed at the idea. But she felt as if it really had happened to her.

They were standing outside an impressive door, thick oak, ornately carved, looking as if it belonged to a royal château. Patrick Delan pressed the doorbell and Rebecca waited, staring impassively at the thick door.

'Smile,' he whispered. 'Florence will be peeping at us through the spy-hole. First impressions are important. . .to Florence,' he added, with a boyish grin.

Rebecca felt she would be damned before she would smile to order! 'Did you forget your key?' she asked.

He shook his head. 'When I said I lived here, I didn't mean actually in this apartment. I live on the top floor. . .always have done since I started working at the Clinique. It's so convenient, being just around the corner.'

Rebecca felt her spirits rise again. How silly of her to jump to conclusions. Not that it was any business of hers what these two got up to.

The door opened and Florence Maurin was framed in a luminous glow from a variety of soft lights in the background of her sumptuous apartment. She raised her delicately boned face and kissed Patrick on both cheeks before berating him for being late.

Rebecca stood poised and ready to be invited in, or, at the very least, to have some acknowledgement of her existence.

'This is Rebecca Manson, our new nursing sister,' Patrick said.

The impeccably manicured hand that took hold of Rebecca's was decidedly limp and the eyes were wary and unfriendly. It was as if Florence Maurin had recognised the rivalry between them even before it had really got started.

Weeks later, Rebecca was to remember this first encounter and wonder how Florence knew what was in store for them. She hadn't planned any of it. . .but it happened just the same. It was fate, destiny—call it what she liked, it was a feeling so powerful that she had no control over it.

CHAPTER THREE

FLORENCE MAURIN threaded her arm through Patrick's and led him into her expensively furnished salon. Rebecca glanced discreetly at the antique *objets d'art* displayed on every available surface as she followed on behind, feeling like a lady in waiting summoned to the royal presence. The heady perfume from the numerous bowls of fresh flowers added to the aura of lavish extravagance. The curtains were cream silk to tone in with the thick carpet. A large, deep, rose-coloured damask-covered sofa, dominating the centre of the room, was surrounded by several exquisitely carved antique chairs and small occasional tables.

Her hostess turned to look at Rebecca and the corners of her thin-lipped mouth twitched into the semblance of a smile.

'Patrick will get you an aperitif,' she announced in her high-pitched, rapid, impeccably Parisian French. 'What would you like?'

Rebecca said the first thing that came into her head. '*Un Ricard, s'il vous plaît, madame.*'

Madame's eyebrows raised ever so slightly. 'Sit down here. I have to see what my maid is getting up to in the kitchen.'

Rebecca sank down amid the cushions of the sofa in the exact spot that Madame Maurin had indicated.

This is ridiculous! she thought to herself as she

31

watched her hostess disappear through an ornately carved archway. I'm behaving like an intimidated schoolgirl. I've got to assert myself. She obviously dislikes me. . . I'm only here on sufferance. She's doing the dutiful thing because Patrick Delan has asked her to. They both feel sorry for the poor little English girl newly arrived in France with no friends.

She sat bolt upright on the edge of the sofa and wondered if she could simply excuse herself now and save them all a lot of embarrassment. She felt sure that Madame Maurin and the doctor would prefer to be alone and decided she must have been mad to accept this invitation.

She half rose, at the same moment as Patrick Delan placed a glass on the table beside her. The arm of her jacket touched against the table and some of the cloudy liquid spilled out on to the drinks mat. Patrick Delan has his white linen handkerchief out in a split second, and Rebecca's startled eyes met his in a long, conspiratorial stare as he mopped at the antique table.

'No harm done,' he said softly.

'Dr Delan. . .' she began slowly.

'Please call me Patrick, and tell me where you learned to drink Ricard.'

He placed the drink she had asked for into her hand. Their fingers touched briefly, and Rebecca gave an involuntary shiver of excitement as she changed her mind and decided to stay on. The ice in her glass gave a musical clinking sound, and suddenly she was transported back in time to that last summer in Brittany, on her grandparents' farm. It was the summer before her grandmother died. She was seven, and wearing her new cotton sundress, the one with the polka-dots and the lacy collar crocheted by her grandmother. She was sitting on her grandfather's knee, intrigued by the smell of his tobacco and the roughness of his weatherbeaten skin.

'It was my grandfather's drink at the end of a day in the fields of his farm,' she said in a far-away voice, almost reluctant to relinquish the mental vision that had sprung up. 'I used to have such a happy time with my grandparents. And I loved to hear the sound of the ice clinking in my grandfather's glass as the sun went down. It meant he would have time to tell me a story and help Grandmaman put me to bed.'

She broke off as she smiled up into Patrick's eyes. He was leaning over her, much longer than was necessary to hand her a drink.

'My grandfather died within weeks of my grandmother. They were inseparable, and I don't think he wanted to live without her. Not like my own parents, who split up the same year. My mother told me she'd known that my grandmother wouldn't live much longer, so she'd persuaded my father to stay until after Grandmaman's death so as not to upset her.'

'And so you didn't come back to France,' Patrick commented, his blue eyes still intently watching her, even though he had moved across the room.

She shook her head. 'We couldn't afford to travel after my father left us. My mother gave private lessons in French, but she didn't earn very much. My father married again and started another family. He always said he couldn't afford to help us out, and my mother didn't insist. She was never strong, and when she caught pneumonia—I was fifteen at the time—she seemed to have lost the will to live, and she just faded away.'

Rebecca's voice had cracked as she recounted the sad story of her mother's unhappy life. Suddenly embarrassed, she glanced up at the doctor, hoping she wasn't being too depressing. 'Look, I don't know why I'm telling you all this. . .'

'It's because you're back in France and all the memories are flooding back,' Patrick said quietly. 'I find it fascinating—but I'm sorry to hear about your mother. Now tell me, where did your grandparents live?'

'In Brittany. They had a farm near St Brieuc.'

'I know the area well—we have a convalescent home on the coast near there. I'll take you down there with me when I next pay them a visit, if you like.'

This time Rebecca was sure her heart had turned over! Yes, there was a definite fluttering in her chest and her breath felt as if it would stop any minute. But her excitement didn't stop her from noticing the elegant figure in the shadows of the doorway.

Florence Maurin stepped forward on her high leather heels and ran long, tapering fingers over her immaculate dark-haired coiffure.

'So you're planning to relocate Sister Manson to Brittany, are you, Patrick?' Without waiting for a reply she turned to Rebecca, a saccharine smile etched into the heavy, flawless make-up. 'You're very fortunate. The convalescent home is delightful, and so much more healthy than being in Paris. I often go down there with Patrick. We take the children for weekends and——'

'Florence, I merely said I would take Rebecca on one of my professional visits. I have no plans to banish her to the country. I can make better use of her medical skills here in Paris.'

Rebecca thought she could feel the temperature drop by ten degrees. The antipathy she had seen in the other woman's attitude changed to barely subdued hostility as she crossed the room and placed a hand on Patrick's arm.

'*Le dîner est servi*,' she told him, in a soft, intimate voice that seemed designed to exclude Rebecca. 'Come with me, Patrick, I want you to help me with the wine.'

Rebecca again found herself following behind her hostess and Patrick. As they moved into the adjoining dining-room, she had time to study the elegant line of Madame Maurin's winter-white cashmere tunic that moulded itself over a pencil-slim black skirt. She was glad she'd worn her suit. No one had asked her if she wanted to take her jacket off; it wasn't that kind of home. Even Patrick was still in the dove-grey designer suit he had been wearing this morning when they first met, with a silk tie firmly knotted in place and not a button disturbed.

She wondered what had happened to the children, and surmised that an unseen maid or nanny must have spirited them away to their bedrooms and insisted on silence so that Maman could entertain.

'Sister Manson can sit over there,' Florence announced, pointing to an intricately carved mahogany antique chair on the hostess's left hand.

Rebecca noticed that Patrick knew his place was beside Florence. She realised that the doctor was the young widow's right-hand man. Without Patrick, Madame Maurin would be unable to function.

Patrick leaned across the table and poured some chilled Chablis into Rebecca's glass before filling his own and raising it to the two ladies.

'*Santé*,' he said, with a polite smile.

Rebecca sipped the white wine and thought how dreadfully formal they were. Was it for her benefit, or did they always spend their evenings like this, just the two of them, after the children had been banished to their rooms? How cosy! She wondered how she'd dared to disrupt their domestic bliss.

And almost guiltily, her thoughts turned to Chris. . .poor Chris, lying there in hospital with his leg in the Thomas's splint. He wouldn't be eating smoked salmon and asparagus spears as she was.

'*Non, merci.*' She shook her head to decline a further helping from Florence Maurin's bone-china serving dish.

The uniformed maid, stiff in her black dress and frilly white apron, placed the main course on the table and retreated into the kitchen. Rebecca had noticed how the young girl's hands shook nervously as she placed the filet mignon in front of her mistress.

There was cheese to follow—some of the delicious Pont l'Evêque that Rebecca had loved as a child. But the effort of standing on ceremony and seemingly playing gooseberry had dulled her appetite. A bowl of fresh fruit appeared, and then finally, when Rebecca knew she couldn't bear another moment of watching Florence Maurin flirting with Patrick Delan, the maid brought in the coffee and it was time to leave the table and go out on to the balcony to sit at a small wrought-iron table overlooking the illuminated private gardens of this prestigious and exclusive apartment block.

Rebecca thought she had never experienced such relief at leaving the dinner table since she was a small child. And she realised she had been made to feel like a child this evening by her hostess. Only occasionally had her remarks been acknowledged, and on a couple of occasions this was only because she had made a grammatical mistake and Madame Maurin had pointedly corrected her.

'It wouldn't matter in the depths of the country, of course, but here in Paris we pride ourselves on the way we speak,' she had said, with the synthetic smile that was beginning to get on Rebecca's nerves.

She looked across the gardens and sipped her coffee, planning to escape at the first possible opportunity. She would politely thank her hostess and walk off around the corner and never. . .never, never return here again. Wild horses wouldn't drag her over the threshold!

Suddenly Madame Maurin's voice interrupted her dark thoughts. 'I have a proposition to put to you, Rebecca. I didn't invite you here simply to be polite.'

You could have fooled me! Rebecca thought acidly.

'A proposition?' she queried out loud.

Madame's smile elongated. 'I have a small *chambre de bonne*. My maid prefers to live out with her boyfriend. . .'

Rebecca noted the disapproval with which this pronouncement was made.

'. . .so my downstairs maid's room is empty. I wondered if you would like to live there while you're working here in Paris.'

Rebecca was taken aback. This *chambre de bonne*, the maid's room, what would it be like? And why was Madame Maurin keen for her to take it? She would have much preferred to live in at the Clinique, but she knew that the private room she had slept in today had only been a temporary arrangement. But she didn't want to be beholden to this woman. She wanted her independence.

Patrick, who so far had remained silent during Florence's proposition, now leaned across the table towards Rebecca.

'I have to say that it's very difficult to find accommodation here in Paris, and the rents are very expensive. You would do well to consider Florence's offer—it's very convenient here for the Clinique.'

Madame Maurin lifted the coffee percolator. 'More coffee, Rebecca?'

Rebecca declined the coffee as she wondered what to do about the *chambre de bonne*. If Patrick hadn't spoken in favour of the situation she would have turned it down flat, but she could see the good points. It was beautifully near to the Clinique, and the less she spent on accommodation the more she could save for her wedding.

Again Florence's voice interrupted her thoughts. 'Of course, I should have to make a tiny, nominal charge for electricity, hot water and so on. And it would help me enormously if you could do the occasional spell of babysitting when the maid can't come in. There's a back staircase that leads directly into my kitchen, so you wouldn't have far to come.'

So that was the catch! Rebecca had sensed there had to be a further fly in the ointment. She was to be relegated to the maid's quarters and called upon to babysit while Florence went out on the tiles with Patrick. Well, thank you, but no, thank you!

As if reading Rebecca's thoughts and before she could decline, Patrick turned to look at their hostess and spoke in a deep, husky, dominating voice.

'The babysitting is out of the question, Florence. Rebecca will be far too busy at the Clinique, and when she's off duty she will need her relaxation.'

Florence's eyes flickered dangerously at this intervention. 'I assure you, Patrick, I will make very few demands in that direction. It will be totally in an emergency capacity. My maid is usually available, but on the odd occasion I need a replacement. And you know how difficult it is to get good babysitters at short notice. Remember what it was like when we went to the ball at the Admiralty. You yourself said——'

'You've missed the point, Florence,' Patrick's voice cut in impatiently. 'I will not have my staff exploited.'

Rebecca drew in her breath nervously as her boss turned towards her. She couldn't help thinking he looked even more handsome when he was angry. But she was glad he wasn't angry with her!

Quite the reverse. As he turned to address her she saw a gentle, tender look assume itself in his expressive blue eyes. 'It's up to you, Rebecca. What do you want to do?'

She knew, beyond a shadow of a doubt, that she

wanted to be near Patrick Delan. And if she had to live in a maid's room, so be it. And if she had to fend off Florence's patronising demands with regard to babysitting, she would do just that.

'I'd like to take the *chambre de bonne*,' she said slowly. 'Perhaps we could have a temporary arrangement. . .say a month's trial. If we both like the arrangement at the end of that time we can continue. If not. . .' She shrugged her shoulders before continuing. 'But I insist on paying my way, Madame Maurin and I must agree on a fixed rent.'

Rebecca saw the look of approval in Patrick's eyes. Almost imperceptibly he nodded before setting down his cup and rising from the table.

'That seems to settle the question, Florence. I'm going to take Rebecca back to the Clinique now—we have an obstetrics case to see to. Rebecca can move in here tomorrow morning. I'll make sure she's free.'

Florence frowned. 'I thought you might like a glass of cognac, Patrick.'

He shook his head. 'Duty calls. I promised the newly delivered mother we'd see her again tonight.'

The atmosphere was decidedly chilly as they said their goodbyes. Once out in the moonlit street, Rebecca breathed a sigh of relief.

She felt Patrick's hand under her arm and her legs started to feel weak again. How to react when she was close to this man was something she would have to learn to handle!

They went in through the revolving door of the Clinique and made their way to the obstetrics unit. Patrick paused outside the door.

'There's no need for you to come in, Rebecca. I promised to check up on our patient, but the night sister can help me. I only brought you back with me because I sensed you'd had enough of Florence. She's not the easiest person to get on with. . .especially if she's. . .' He paused, as if searching for the right words.

Rebecca was aware of the throbbing of the air-conditioning. Somewhere close by in one of the Clinique rooms, a patient was loudly snoring. All the nocturnal hospital sounds were around her, the atmosphere she knew so well in her medical world. But she'd never met a doctor like this before. She'd never been so moved, physically and emotionally.

'Especially if she's what?' she prompted softly.

He stared down at her, his eyes full of a deep tenderness as he put a long, tapering finger under her chin so that she was forced to look up at him.

'Especially if she's jealous,' he murmured quietly. 'She can be very demanding with me. Unfortunately, I have become the centre of her world.'

'So I noticed,' Rebecca said crisply. 'But I can't see why she could possibly be jealous of me.'

'Don't you?' he queried softly. 'I do.'

And then he stooped down and kissed her.

Her legs turned to jelly as his lips claimed hers. Instinctively she knew she mustn't give any indication of her feelings. She mustn't show how moved she was.

She tried to move away, but his arms pulled her into a firm embrace. Her eyes had closed at the touch of his kiss, but now she opened them and stared up at him.

He was so different from Chris. . .she knew now that her eyes had closed because she felt guilty.

'No,' she murmured against Patrick's lips, and immediately he released his hold on her.

There was a strange, enigmatic smile on his face as he cupped her chin with his hands. 'This is why Florence was jealous of you,' he whispered. 'Because she could see that I was attracted to you. I didn't have to tell her any more than I had to tell you. Words are unimportant in a situation like this. . . Do you believe in love at first sight, Rebecca?'

Her thoughts were in turmoil as she stepped backwards, away from him, leaning heavily against the wall of the corridor so that she could steady herself.

'I'm very inexperienced,' she said quietly. 'And I'm already engaged to someone who needs me.'

Patrick kept his distance. They were a couple of yards apart now, but Rebecca was still painfully aware of his magnetic attraction as he leaned towards her.

'You haven't replied to my question, but I think you're afraid to give an answer. You're not free any more than I am. We both have our commitments, so the question is purely academic. I merely wanted to know if you felt the same as I do. But either way, we can do nothing about it. We're not free agents, so we can't give in to any romantic notions.'

She raised her eyes once more to his face and saw the deep tenderness in his eyes.

'Did anyone ever tell you your hazel eyes reflect the gold in your hair?' he asked.

She smiled, feeling a surge of pure joy deep inside

her. 'I thought you said we should banish romantic notions, Dr Delan.'

He laughed, a rich, boyish sound that elevated her spirits even more.

'We can try,' he said, in a husky voice that was totally devoid of conviction.

CHAPTER FOUR

REBECCA had found it impossible to sleep. She had tossed and turned in her bed in the Clinique room, longing for the beginning of the new day.

She could hardly believe it was only twenty-four hours since she'd arrived in Paris. As she rose from her bed to pull open the long velvet curtains, she felt it was incredible that her life could have taken on such a new dimension. Through the billowing net of the window curtains she could see the cleansing lorry trundling along the street spraying out water. A tiny pampered poodle yelped and leapt back into its mistress's arms as the particles of water reached the pavement.

She turned back into the room, remembering that this time yesterday she hadn't even met Patrick Delan. And yet she'd spent all night thinking about him. True, her body had been out of synchronisation due to her having slept all day after delivering the new baby. But she'd never had a problem with adjusting to day or night duty. She'd always been able to sleep as soon as her head touched the pillow. Her colleagues in the nurses' home back in London had told her it was because she led an innocent life and had no guilty secrets to keep her awake.

But not any more! She sat down on the edge of the bed, pulling the old dressing-gown around her. It was like a familiar teddy bear, the sort of comfort-deriving object she had turned to as a child when there was a situation she didn't understand. . .like when her parents were having one of their frightening rows.

She was wondering how she could allow these romantic feelings for her new boss even to enter her thoughts, let alone dwell on them for a whole night, when the bedside phone rang. It was the all-night receptionist giving her a morning call.

'*Merci*. . . I'm awake,' Rebecca replied, running a hand through her rumpled red hair.

'Dr Delan has requested that you begin your morning in the obstetrics unit,' the receptionist informed her.

She was even more awake now! Even the sound of his name sent shivers down her spine.

As she showered and dressed, she wondered if it was because she was totally devoid of experience other than with Chris. Most girls of twenty-five had experienced more than one boyfriend. Her own mother had told her, during one of their girly chats, that she'd enjoyed the romantic attentions of numerous beaux during her student days in Paris, before she had met Rebecca's father. But somehow Rebecca had stuck with Chris because she had come to think that loyalty was one of the most important aspects of life. If somebody loved and needed you, you had to stick by them. . .not like her father, who'd broken her mother's heart with his philandering.

She clasped the silver buckle at her waist and glanced at her reflection in the mirror as she brushed out her long hair. She had her father's colouring; the red, fiery hair was from her tall, thickset Scottish father, not her

demure, tiny, dark-haired French mother. She had
always wondered if she had inherited his temperament,
and that was why she'd fought so hard against any
feelings that might be disloyal to Chris.

There'd been that time at the nurses' home
Christmas ball, when one of the junior doctors whom
she'd secretly fancied had made a pass at her. She had
rebuffed him, of course, but Chris had noticed and
made a scene in the middle of the dance-floor. She
could feel her cheeks burning as she remembered the
humiliation. And Chris had made her life hell for the
next few weeks. Always a jealous person, he'd really
gone over the top that time, she remembered. And she
had decided then and there that it wasn't worth the
hassle. She had always been Chris's girl and he would
be heartbroken. . .just as her mother had been when
her father left home. . .if she were to try to change the
situation.

She screwed her hair up on top and pinned the tiny
white cap on her head. Oh, come on, where's your
sense of proportion? she asked herself, pulling a wry
face at her reflection. It was the lack of sleep that was
affecting her; she was over-reacting to a particularly
sympathetic doctor who had turned her head at an
especially vulnerable time.

As she went out of the door, she tried to convince
herself that things would be different in the clear light
of day.

But as she went through the door of the first room in
the obstetrics unit and saw Patrick Delan leaning over
their patient's bed she knew that nothing had changed.

Her feelings were the same as they had been last night. . .but even more confused!

He turned at the sound of her footsteps and gave her a long, lingering smile.

'I see you got my message, Sister Manson.'

'Yes, Doctor.' Her heart was beating rapidly, but she knew if she could keep up the professional relationship she might be able to ignore her romantic feelings.

He turned back to look at their patient. 'Jane's had a good night. The night nurse gave Baby his feeds during the night, but it's time to get on with some more breast feeding. Jane's very keen to feed if she can, so I'd like you to give her some help and encouragement.'

'Of course.' Rebecca avoided his eyes as she smiled down at their patient.

'And then I'd like you to come along to my office,' he added quietly.

His voice was totally professional, but the look in his eyes was otherwise. There was a hint of the tenderness she'd seen the night before, and she didn't know if she was going to be able to handle it.

'Yes, sir,' she replied in a deliberately light tone.

Before she turned to attend to her patient she saw the boyish smile on Patrick Delan's lips. He wasn't taken in by her attempt at resolving the situation any more than she was.

She heard the sound of the outer door swinging to as she bent over Jane Gordon. He was gone, so now she could get on with her nursing duties and very soon her pulse would stop pounding—she hoped!

'It's all very new to me, Sister, this idea that I'm responsible for another life,' Jane Gordon said, in an apprehensive voice. 'I've had forty-two years in which to look after myself totally, so, I don't mind telling you, I suddenly feel very scared.'

Rebecca gave her patient a reassuring smile. 'That's perfectly natural, Jane. I should feel exactly the same myself after only twenty-five years. It's hard to feel responsible for someone else. But I think you'll make such a good mother, because you're totally committed. Now, let me put your lovely son into your arms, like so. . .'

Rebecca lifted the sweet-smelling, new-born infant from his crib and handed him over to his mother, telling her just how wonderful she thought he was.

'Have you chosen a name yet?' she asked.

The mother smiled. 'We're going to call him Patrick after the man who brought him into the world. I knew just as soon as I started ante-natal examinations with Dr Delan that I wanted to remember him. He really is a remarkable doctor, don't you think?'

Rebecca swallowed hard as she willed herself to remain calm. 'I've only just met him, so I really couldn't say. I—er—I enjoyed working with him yesterday. . .Now, young Patrick, your mother and I want you to catch on to this nipple, like this. . .'

With gentle fingers Rebecca coaxed the baby's mouth, and within seconds he was feeding as if it was the most natural thing in the world. . .which in fact it was, as Rebecca reminded the new mother.

'So far so good. . .but don't leave me, Sister,' Jane Gordon said cautiously, as she looked down at her son with unbelieving eyes.

Rebecca sat down on the edge of the bed and patted

her patient's hand. 'You're doing remarkably well for a first-time mum.'

Jane smiled. 'It's like a miracle! Two years ago I wasn't married or even thinking about it. I was the ultimate career woman, completely self-sufficient and totally happy with my lifestyle. And then along came my gorgeous husband and turned my well-ordered life upside down. Do you believe in love at first sight, Sister?'

Oh, no, not the same question again! Rebecca drew in her breath as she tried to look as if she were considering the idea from an academic point of view.

'Do you?' she countered, feeling at a loss for an answer.

'Oh, yes,' Jane Gordon replied dreamily. 'It really is the most wonderful feeling in the world. I was totally bowled over. Brian just walked into my office one day. . . I was director of personnel in a computer firm. He looked across my desk and asked me something about work. I can't even remember what it was all about, because my legs suddenly felt weak and wobbly. If you haven't experienced it, Sister, you'll think I'm mad! Anyway, that was the moment that changed my life. He asked me out to lunch, and we were married three months later.'

'It sounds so romantic. . .come on, little fellow, don't go to sleep.' Rebecca gently urged the tiny rosebud mouth to continue sucking, knowing that if she concentrated on her nursing duties the romantic ideas would disappear. Her patient had described exactly how she felt about Patrick Delan—that meteoric soaring of the spirits, the inexplicable surge of *joie de vivre*. . .

'Are you married, Sister? I know you don't wear a ring, but that doesn't mean a thing these days.'

'I'm engaged,' Rebecca replied cautiously. 'I haven't got a ring because my fiancé decided it would be better to save the money in a building society. He's very practical and he couldn't see the point of wasting——'

'Oh, I entirely agree,' Jane interrupted. 'When you're young, you haven't had time to save up like us old ones. Now, forgive me if I'm poking my nose in, but I just had the feeling then that you would have liked to have a ring. . .and hang the expense.'

Rebecca smiled, and a far-away look came into her eyes. 'It's not so much the ring I would have liked as a little more romantic attention. We women set more store by these things than the men, don't you think?'

Mrs Gordon hesitated. 'Look, I'm old enough to give you the benefit of my wealth of experience with numerous boyfriends. If the man in your life doesn't make you feel special. . .then forget him! If you don't get a thrill every time he comes near you, you're with the wrong man.'

The patient broke off with a gentle laugh that seemed designed to defuse the tension caused by her remarks. 'Look, I probably know more about these things than you do, but you certainly know more about the medical world. So it's time for me to ask your advice. How long do you think I should stay here in the Clinique? Brian is dying to have me home again, but I don't know if I can cope with this new little stranger in our lives in the outside world. Dr Delan has suggested I stay for a week.'

'Then I think you should take the doctor's advice,' Rebecca told her, as she took hold of the infant and transferred him to the patient's other breast. 'There, your baby's going to be no problem at all, and you're a born mother. Do you have any domestic help?'

'Oh, yes; I've got a live-in maid, and a daily *femme de ménage*,' said Mrs Gordon, smiling down fondly at her suckling infant.

'Then you're going to be fine. You can concentrate on the baby—and your husband—and leave the domestic chores to the paid help.'

Rebecca changed the baby's nappy at the end of the feed and settled him in his crib at the side of the bed.

'I've got to leave you now,' she told her patient.

Jane Gordon reached out and touched her arm. 'You're going to see Dr Delan, aren't you?'

'Yes, we're having a meeting. I expect he's going to brief me about today's schedule, so I mustn't keep him waiting.'

The patient's fingers tightened on her arm. 'You may be able to fool yourself, Sister, but you don't fool me. . .either of you. I could sense the chemistry between you two even yesterday during my delivery. And this morning, when you walked in through that door, I saw the effect you had on Dr Delan. Now, I've lived in Paris long enough to hear all the gossip, and that woman he's protecting has got too much of a hold on him. That wonderful man never stood a chance after his wife died. He needs someone in his life who's sympathetic. . .someone he can love for love's sake only, not out of a sense of duty. . .someone like——'

'Jane, I have to go now,' Rebecca cut short the words that she didn't want to hear, the words that were upsetting her more than she cared to admit. 'I'll be back later.'

Rebecca's heart was thumping madly as she went out through the swing doors. If Jane Gordon hadn't been a patient, she would have told her to mind her own business. How dared she add to the problem?

But as she walked along the corridor, Jane's words were pounding through her head. 'For love's sake only.'

Oh, wouldn't it be wonderful to have a truly unfettered relationship. . .to love someone because you really wanted to. . .not just from a sense of duty? But romantic love only happened in books and films. In real life there were far too many mundane considerations. . .and yet her patient claimed that she was still madly in love with the father of her baby.

She had reached Patrick Delan's office, and now she tapped lightly on the door. He opened it and held it wide open, an enigmatic smile on his face.

'Come in, Sister Manson. How did the feeding session go?'

Rebecca noticed a medical secretary rising from the seat beside the doctor's desk, murmuring that she would return to finish the correspondence later when *monsieur le docteur* was again free.

'Jane Gordon is a natural mother and there are no problems with the feeding. But I've endorsed your recommendation that she stay on for a week,' said

Rebecca. 'Even though her domestic arrangements are excellent, she needs to build up her strength before going home.'

Patrick motioned her to sit down in the chair vacated by the medical secretary. 'I'm glad we agree on that point.'

He ran a hand through his short hair, and Rebecca sensed that he was uncharacteristically nervous.

'I've had a telephone call,' he began, his blue eyes on her face. 'It appears that there's a medical problem in the Brittany nursing home that the staff can't handle. I've decided to go down there at the weekend. Would you like to come with me?'

Would she? With all her heart she longed to say yes, but she was afraid of her feelings. . .afraid she wouldn't be able to handle them if she was alone with Patrick Delan for any length of time.

'Do you need me to help you?' she asked cautiously, as she played for time.

A flicker of a frown crossed his face. 'I can understand that you might prefer to spend your first weekend seeing the bright lights of Paris.'

'But do you need my services?' She was saying her piece, salving her conscience and hating the inner turmoil of her thoughts. A weekend in Brittany would be so wonderful! To see the places she had known as a child. . .and to be accompanied by this man who was playing havoc with her emotions in a way she'd never experienced.

'We're not short-staffed down there, if that's what you mean. But I thought it would be an opportunity of showing you the medical facilities we have on offer.

And I must admit I do get lonely driving there by myself. A young, amusing companion wouldn't go amiss.'

She saw the twinkle in his eyes and decided not to be so churlish. She could think of nothing else she would like better than a weekend in the country. Why spoil it by listening to her over-active conscience?

She smiled. 'Well, if you put it like that, how can I refuse?'

CHAPTER FIVE

EARLY on Saturday morning, as Patrick drove off the Périphérique, the road that encircled Paris, and headed the car towards the south-west, Rebecca breathed a sigh of relief. There had been times during the past couple of days when she'd thought they would never make it!

First there had been the phone call from Chris, asking when she was going to go back to London for a weekend. He was feeling lonely after only a few days without her. She had explained that she couldn't go back to England for a few weeks until she'd fully settled into her new job. Chris had then come back with the plan that maybe he could be transferred to her clinic as soon as he came off the traction. She had told him that the fees were astronomical—way above anything he could afford. At the end of the phone call she assured him she would try to get over to see him before Christmas. 'Christmas!' he'd exploded down the phone.

Now, as she gazed out of the window, in the fast lane of the *autoroute*, her eyes barely registered the cars they were passing. The problem of Chris travelled with her and couldn't be shaken off. Unconsciously she gave a big sigh.

'You sound as if you've got the cares of the world on

your shoulders,' Patrick commented, without taking his eyes from the busy road as he negotiated a bend.

Rebecca shook herself. 'Oh, it's nothing I can't handle. It's only that, now I've got time to think about it, I feel I may have been a bit unsympathetic.'

'I take it we're talking about that phone call you got from your fiancé?' he asked mildly.

She stared at him in surprise. 'How did you know?'

He laughed. 'I think the whole of the Clinique noticed your uncharacteristic bad temper yesterday afternoon. But it was Jane Gordon who reported the details to me. I don't know why she thought I should know about it.'

Rebecca gritted her teeth. It had been so unfortunate that the phone call had been put through to the obstetrics unit and her patient had listened in to the whole conversation.

'Jane Gordon has taken on a sort of elder sister role with me,' she explained. 'She perceives me as being naïve where men are concerned, and. . .'

'And are you?'

Rebecca hesitated. 'Well, I've made a point of staying faithful to the same person for a number of years, and——'

'Why? Do you love him?'

She took a deep breath. 'My feelings have got nothing to do with anyone but myself. I believe in keeping promises, in being faithful, in——'

'OK, OK! I only asked. There's no need to bite my head off! So long as he makes you happy there's no problem. But Jane said you were worried about his hospital treatment. Apparently he's coming off traction soon. If it would make you any happier, we could treat him out here. I've got an excellent orthopaedic unit in Brittany. Chris could be nursed at the convalescent home.'

'It's out of the question. He couldn't afford——'

'I would take him free of charge, as a concession to one of my employees. It's all part of the service to keep my staff happy. If you're worrying about something, you're not going to do your job very well. Now, let's stop off for a coffee at this service station. And for heaven's sake, try to forget your problems, Rebecca.'

'You're very kind,' she murmured, as the car came to a halt in front of a glass-fronted, high-roofed building. The thought that Chris could come out to join her should have made her feel better. She was even trying to convince herself that it did. But the surge of excitement she felt was simply because Patrick Delan had leapt out of the car and come around to hold open her door, his hand gently steadying her arm.

She wasn't used to these gallant gestures of concern. The polite courtesy of this Parisian doctor was like wine. It went to her head and made her feel intoxicated.

They didn't linger over their coffee, Patrick having made it clear that he wanted to reach La Colombière, his convalescent nursing home, by lunchtime. But he insisted she give him an answer to his offer of a place for Chris.

She looked around the spotless service station, unconsciously comparing it with some of the motorway cafés she'd visited in England, sipping at her strong percolated coffee in its tiny blue china cup while she searched her heart for the right answer. Chris would be over the moon; it would speed his recovery; Patrick seemed to want it; perhaps, like herself, he felt they should cool their heady relationship and come down to earth. . .recognise their responsibilities.

He leaned forward and took the cup from her hand, placing it down on the table as he looked directly into her troubled hazel eyes.

'Why so glum? I thought this was what you wanted?'

'Oh, it is!' she said, in what was meant to be a convincing voice. 'I'm deeply grateful, and I know Chris will be when I tell him.'

Patrick flashed her a brilliant smile. 'Good. Then that's settled and you can come back from wherever you've been for the past twenty-four hours.'

They were back in the car within minutes, hurtling along the autoroute. Rebecca found a sudden, unexpected calm descending upon her. It was almost as if fate had stepped in and made a decision for her. It was also the fact that in a few short hours she would be nearing the part of France that she knew so well from her infancy.

She closed her eyes; the early morning start had meant only a few hours' sleep. The leather seat was so comfortable and the car ran so smoothly. In no time at all, she lapsed into a deep sleep.

'We're almost there. Wake up, sleepyhead!'

Patrick's voice interrupted her dreams. She'd been back on her grandparents' farm, asking them if she could bring her new boyfriend to lunch. In the dream she was a very small girl again, and now, as she woke

up, she had absolutely no recollection of who the new
boyfriend had been. . .but he'd certainly been there in
her dreams. And she had a shrewd suspicion of who
she'd been dreaming about!

She rubbed her eyes as she tried to come back to
reality. Patrick took his eyes off the road for a split
second and she saw the tender expression. She wondered if he had been observing her while she slept, and
hoped she hadn't snored!

'Have I been asleep long?' she asked.

He laughed. 'Ages! Some companion you turned out
to be!'

'Where are we?' Rebecca pushed the hair out of her
eyes as she stared out of the window.

'We're very near to the Brittany coast—west of St
Brieuc,' he told her.

'Never! The roads have changed so much!' she
exclaimed, as Patrick accelerated over the wide dual
carriageway that bypassed St Brieuc. 'This used to be
such a bumpy, narrow road. I remember travelling
along here in my grandpa's ancient Citroën—it was
like something out of a Maigret film. And we went so
slowly, but there was no chance of anyone passing us
on the narrow stretch of road that led into the town.
They used to honk their horns, but my grandfather
took no notice. He went even slower, if anything, just
to annoy them.'

Patrick took a sideways glance at her. 'You sound
very fond of the old man.'

She swallowed the lump in her throat. 'He was the
only real father I ever knew. My own father was. . .'

Rebecca's voice cracked as it always did when she

thought about the misery her father had inflicted on the family. Suddenly Patrick's hand had left the steering-wheel and was covering her own.

'It's OK. You don't have to tell me,' he murmured. 'I understand. When we've got time, we'll go and have a look at your grandparents' farm. But we've got to make it out to La Colombière for lunch or Matron will never forgive me.'

The convalescent nursing home was perched high on a hill overlooking wide, sandy beaches on either side of the headland. As the car ground to a halt on the gravel drive by the front door, Rebecca jumped out to look at the view. She was so excited she didn't even give Patrick time to open her door.

'I'm sure I remember that beach,' she said, pointing down the cliff. 'That's where Grandmaman used to leave me at the Club Mickey when she did her shopping up in the village. Isn't that an incredible coincidence? I used to look up at this beautiful house and wonder who lived in it.'

Patrick put a hand on her shoulder protectively. 'Be careful you don't go too near the edge. I can tell you who lived in this house. It's been in my family for generations. When I was a boy we lived in Paris, but we always came down here for holidays and some long weekends.'

Rebecca's eyes opened wide in disbelief. 'So many coincidences! We share so many situations. We may have met on the beach as children. . .' She broke off with a smile. 'I'm forgetting the age difference. You wouldn't look at a young girl when you were in your teens, would you?'

The hand on her shoulder tightened. 'If she were as pretty as you I would. Come on, let's go inside.'

'Wait! Just one more moment while I look down on the beach. It's like going back in time. Nothing has changed!' She turned her face up to his. 'When did you turn your house into a nursing home?'

'Soon after I qualified. My parents had died the previous summer.' Patrick hesitated as his eyes swept out over the panoramic view. Slowly he raised his hand and pointed out to sea. 'They were out there in the worst storm for years in our yacht. It was a beautiful old pre-war boat, made of wood.'

He turned away his head so that Rebecca couldn't see the expression on his face. 'My father loved that boat. He used to take me with him when I was quite small, I remember. . .'

Rebecca heard the emotional catch in his voice and remained silent.

'My father was an experienced sailor—it was only a hobby, of course. Whenever he could get down here from his medical practice in Paris, he would escape on to the water. On this occasion he'd taken my mother with him. The storm blew up very quickly, as often happens along this coast. The *canot de sauvetage* set out to help them after receiving their distress call on the radio, but the boat had capsized and begun to sink. My parents' bodies were washed up later on the shore.'

Rebecca drew in her breath. 'I'm so sorry. Does it bring back memories. . .whenever you come down here?'

'Only happy ones,' he told her, smiling down at her, as if to show that he had no place for sadness in his life. 'We were always a close, happy family, so that's what I remember. In my father's will he asked that this house should be used as a nursing home and that I should be the Medical Director after I qualified. He'd set up a charitable medical trust which benefited from his work in Paris, so I was able to go ahead with no financial worries. La Colombière became financially independent, so I decided to buy the Clinique Ste-Catherine. I don't mind admitting that financial matters bore me—I leave it all to my accountant, who advises me what I can and can't afford to do. He's been with the family for years. But if I decide that a patient needs treatment they can't afford, I go ahead with it anyway. Small matters like that are easy to handle.'

She looked up into his eyes and saw her own concern reflected there. 'That's what you're doing about Chris, isn't it?'

He nodded. 'A worthy case, if ever there was one. . .if it will make you happy. . .now come along inside and meet the staff.'

They were barely through the wide oak door before a large, plump lady in navy blue bore down upon them, a beaming smile on her friendly face. She greeted Patrick with kisses on both cheeks and loud exclamations of delight.

Rebecca gathered that they had waited lunch so that Patrick could sit at the head of the staff table as host. And the staff were starving after a long morning's work!

Patrick introduced Rebecca to Madame Thiret as they were swept along on a voluble French tide towards the dining-room. Rebecca assumed that this had to be the matron in charge of the establishment, and found herself warming to her. She knew she wouldn't mind working with a woman like this—salt of the earth—if ever she was sent down here. But for the moment she was more than happy in Paris.

Her eyes swept around the large dining-room, making an unconscious comparison with the dingy basement canteen at St Celine's in London. The whole of one side was given over to large casement windows through which could be seen the blue September sky and the breathtakingly beautiful wide sweep of the bay, with her childhood beach tucked into one corner.

There were welcoming cries from the staff assembled on each side of a long oak refectory table as Patrick took his place at the head, motioning to Rebecca to sit beside him. This entailed moving one of the pale-blue-uniformed sisters one place lower down the table, but she didn't seem to mind. Like the matron, this sister had the healthy glow often found in countrywomen—plump pink cheeks and a wide smile that revealed strong white teeth.

Patrick introduced Rebecca over the hubbub of French chatter as his new English sister in Paris. There were murmurs of approval, but the young physiotherapist at the end of the table commented to another colleague that she thought the red-haired sister was too petite to cope with the job of sister. Rebecca hastily joined in the conversation to show that she could speak French and avoid any other comments that she wasn't supposed to hear!

As she glanced sideways down the table she saw that the physiotherapist was blushing as she bent her head over the plate of oysters in front of her. She felt sorry for the girl's *faux pas*. She looked a friendly sort of person, probably the impulsive type who spoke before she thought! Her long blonde hair was tied at the back in a neat blue ribbon, and, even sitting down, it was easy to see that she was of statuesque dimensions— positively Amazonian, Rebecca decided. So she would be the sort of person who couldn't comprehend that small girls could be strong.

Patrick noticed the girl's embarrassment and called down the table to her. 'Don't worry, Karine; Sister Manson is used to hearing comments about her size, but, I can assure you, she's very tough and can hold her own against people who are twice the size.'

Rebecca flashed him a grateful smile, before turning her attention on the starter. 'Oysters for lunch. . . I can't believe this is an everyday lunch. Aren't they expensive?'

Patrick laughed. 'Not round here. You've forgotten your childhood, I suspect.'

The main course was *coq au vin*, followed by a salad tossed in a herb-flavoured vinaigrette, and then they had *tarte aux pommes*.

After the meal, Rebecca was taken on a guided tour of the large, high-ceilinged rooms that had been converted into small surgical, orthopaedic, and medical units.

'It has a lovely atmosphere,' she remarked to Madame Thiret as she found herself and Patrick ensconced in the kindly matron's room at the end of the tour. 'It's very obvious that it was once a private house. . .a family home.'

Madame Thiret beamed. 'This is what we've always tried to maintain. I had the privilege of being house-keeper to Patrick's parents. I'd previously trained as a nurse, but Dr Delan senior persuaded me to take up the housekeeping position, saying that he needed someone who understood the medical world and could take messages and so on when the family was in Paris. So I stayed on, and then, after the tragic shipwreck, Patrick asked me to take charge of the nursing side of La Colombière. I'm very much an administrator now-adays, but I do manage some real nursing occasionally.'

Patrick leaned forward. 'More than occasionally, by all accounts. It's time you were taking things easy. Let the younger staff do the work, Marie.'

Madame Thiret smiled happily. 'You spoil me.'

'No, I don't. I'm merely being grateful for everything you've done for me over the years. . .even the times when you scolded me when I was a child!'

All three of them laughed. Rebecca leaned back in the soft cretonne-covered armchair and looked out of the window. The sky was still blue. She hoped there would be time for a walk on the beach before the sun went down.

'And now tell me about this problem you have, Marie,' Patrick began, in a suddenly uncharacteristi-cally solemn voice.

CHAPTER SIX

MADAME THIRET looked suddenly flustered. 'I'm sorry to have dragged you all this way down, Patrick. I suppose I could have discussed it with you over the phone. . .but then you never know who's listening, do you?'

Rebecca could sense a certain impatience as Patrick stood up and walked over to the window of the matron's office. 'You're being very mysterious, Marie. I assure you it's no hardship to come down to this part of the country after the hustle and bustle of life in Paris.'

He partially turned and gave Rebecca a smile before continuing. 'I needed to escape for a weekend to recharge the batteries, so tell me what it is you want me to do so that I can get it out of the way and enjoy myself. I want to have time to take Rebecca down to the beach where she used to play as a child, and——'

'Well, it's more of an administrative problem, really,' Marie Thiret broke in quickly. 'You see, the accountant has been insisting that we stay within our budget. Now, the level of fees he advised last year is way above what many of our patients can afford. Many patients discharge themselves before they're fit. . .and some patients don't even start treatment because they know they won't be able to afford our fees.'

Patrick frowned as he strode back across the room

to resume his seat between Rebecca and Madame Thiret. 'You should know me well enough by now, Marie. When a patient requires treatment he should be treated, regardless of whether he can afford our private fees or not. My father wanted this place to become a haven for sick people who needed medical care—that was why he set up the trust in Paris and turned over all his assets there. As a family we've always had more than enough money to finance our medical concerns, and it's a well-known fact that money breeds money. Our accountant has invested wisely and the medical trust has prospered, so that——'

'You try telling that to Monsieur Fromentin!' Madame Thiret interrupted fiercely. 'He's instructed me not to admit any more non-fee-paying patients until after his next consultation with you.' She paused and looked warily at Patrick. 'So I thought I'd speak to you first and get you on my side. I was born and bred around here, and I like to think that La Colombière is a very special place where my fellow-countrymen can come when their health is failing. Because, you see, we're the only hospital for miles around where alternative and orthodox medicine can go hand in hand.'

Patrick gave the older woman a broad smile. 'Ah, so now we come to the crux of the matter. Jacques Fromentin doesn't approve of some of our new methods, does he?' He waved his arm expansively. 'But you're in charge here, Marie, and I'm in control of the finances. I'll speak to Jacques when I get back to Paris and make sure he doesn't go over my head again. We can afford to be generous to our patients who can't pay the fees. No deserving case should be turned away.'

He paused, and his eyes dwelled on Rebecca's face. 'Within the next two or three months, Rebecca's fiancé will be coming over from England, and I'd like him to receive the best attention possible. He's recovering from a fractured femur and he'll need lots of physio-therapy. I think we'll assign Karine Griffon to him. She's very firm with her patients and she gets excellent results.'

Madame Thiret smiled at her boss. 'Yes, I'm very pleased with Karine. Although she's only twenty-five, she works as if she's had years of experience. Now, tell me about Sister's fiancé. Will he be coming straight here from England?'

Patrick shook his head. 'There'll be a short period at the Clinique Ste-Catherine for me to assess his treat-ment, and then he'll come down for his convalescence. I expect Rebecca will want to transfer down here.'

'I hope she does,' said Madame Thiret. 'We're going to be short-staffed if we start expanding in the way you've just outlined, Patrick.'

'You can certainly twist my words, Marie!' Patrick said, with a bemused expression on his face. 'There's no need to go mad with admissions—always check with me first—but don't turn anyone away unless I decide they could be best treated elsewhere.'

Madame Thiret beamed happily. 'Now, let me make some more coffee.'

'*Non, merci.*' Patrick had got to his feet and was holding out his hand towards Rebecca. 'I want to take Sister for a walk—the fresh air will do her good. It's been so stuffy in Paris for the past few days.'

Rebecca thought she saw a secret smile on the older

woman's face as Patrick's hand claimed her own. Someone else sizing up the situation! she thought. It must be difficult for people not to notice the way she felt about Patrick.

'This fiancé of yours,' Madame Thiret began. 'When's the wedding?'

Rebecca turned at the door, putting a smile on her face that didn't convince anyone, least of all herself. 'We've had to postpone our plans since my fiancé's accident,' she said.

'Well, don't worry, my dear. He'll be in good hands even if you don't come down here with him.'

'Oh, I expect she will,' Patrick said firmly, as he held open the door.

The sun was dipping slowly behind the hill on top of which was perched La Colombière. Looking up now at the grey and white building, Rebecca thought she had never seen it looking so lovely. Years ago, as a child, she had invented secret stories about the place. To her, it had been a fairy-tale castle—and once she'd imagined she was the princess who lived there with servants to wait on her and lots of friends of her own age to play with. . .

'You're far away again!' Patrick's bemused voice broke through her reverie.

She laughed and turned to look at him. They were lying on the warm sand. Patrick had spread his jacket down for her, while he was propped against the dark grey boulders that encircled the bay. For several minutes neither of them had spoken, both seemingly absorbed in their own thoughts.

'I was remembering how it used to be. . .all my childish dreams.'

'I expect you were waiting for a handsome prince to come along and sweep you away on a white charger,' he laughed.

She shook her head. 'No, I wasn't that sophisticated at eight years old. I would have settled for the boy next door if he'd bought me an ice-cream.'

'And you did settle for the boy next door,' he murmured, leaning up on one arm to look down at her.

She sat up quickly, feeling the bonhomie evaporate. 'Not quite. Chris and I were at school together, but we lived several miles apart.'

'I think it will be best if you transfer down here when Chris comes out to France,' said Patrick, in a firm tone. 'That way, the problem will resolve itself.'

Their eyes met. 'What problem?' Rebecca asked.

He leaned forward and kissed her gently on the lips. 'This problem,' he told her, as he pulled himself away.

She turned away, staring out to sea through misted eyes. Why did life have to be so complicated? Why was she committed to someone else, and why had she fallen in love with a man who wasn't free?

She turned back and saw that Patrick was looking down at her. He reached out his hand, and as he took hold of hers she gave an involuntary shiver.

'It's getting cold out here; we should be moving back up the hill,' he murmured softly.

Their eyes met and she saw the troubled expression in his. She wondered if he was wishing she were free. But no, he couldn't be thinking that. He was making

plans for Chris to join them in France. He was doing
the decent thing—killing the romance before it started.

She jumped to her feet, picking up Patrick's jacket
and vigorously brushing away the sand. One of the tiny
particles must have jumped into her eye, because she
felt a sharp stabbing pain.

He was instantly by her side, taking her by the
shoulders and examining the offending eye. 'Hold still,
Rebecca, I can see the problem.'

She remained motionless as he fished out his handkerchief and deftly removed the tiny speck of sand.

'Thanks very much. I'm glad I had my own personal
doctor with me,' she said, in a bantering tone.

His hands were still on her shoulders and he was
looking down at her with an expression of deep tenderness. 'I love taking care of you, Rebecca,' he said
huskily.

And then suddenly his arms were around her and
she was being pulled into his strong embrace. He bent
his head and kissed her with a surging passion. This
time she didn't close her eyes; she wanted to know that
it was Patrick. And as she moved against him, revelling
in the strength of his hard, muscular body, she knew
that the romantic feelings she was experiencing
couldn't be wrong. Falling in love with Patrick seemed
the most sane thing she had ever done in her life.

Afterwards, she had no idea how long she had
remained in his arms. As they walked back up the hill,
hand in hand, she found herself wishing that the
romantic idyll could have gone on forever.

The sun had disappeared behind the hill when they

reached La Colombière. Some of the off-duty staff
were sitting on the stone patio at the front of the house,
sipping aperitifs before *le dîner*. Rebecca noticed
Karine, the young physiotherapist who had put her
foot in it at the lunch table. The blonde girl waved to
them and suggested a drink.

Patrick shook his head. 'Later, Karine. I've promised
Madame Thiret I'll do the evening round of the patients
with her. But Rebecca can join you if she likes.'

Rebecca looked questioningly at Patrick. 'You're
sure you don't need me?'

His eyes danced mischievously. 'That's an ambiguous
question, Rebecca,' he whispered, in English.

She blushed and turned away. 'I'll go and have that
drink with Karine.'

'I'll join you later,' Patrick told her.

'Come and sit here, Sister,' the physiotherapist
called. 'Let me get you an aperitif. We're all drinking
Kir this evening.'

'*Vous êtes très gentille,*' Rebecca said as she sat down
on one of the wrought-iron chairs next to Karine, who
introduced her to two young doctors and a couple of
nurses.

There was a bottle of white wine and a bottle of
crème de cassis—blackcurrant liqueur—on the table,
and one of the doctors, a dark-haired young man by
the name of Edouard Sabatier, mixed a Kir for
Rebecca, handing it to her with a friendly smile.

'Welcome to La Colombière,' he said. 'Will you be
coming to work down here with us?'

She took a sip of the refreshing drink. 'I think I
might,' she replied. 'My fiancé is going to come out

here as a patient soon, so Patrick Delan has very kindly suggested I might like a transfer.'

'It's not as exciting as Paris, but it has its compensations,' Karine Griffon put in. 'I'm really sorry I made derogatory remarks about you at lunchtime,' she added, with a wry grin. 'To be honest, I've always wished I were smaller. I've inherited these long legs from my Swedish mother, and I'd love to be petite like you.'

Rebecca laughed. 'We always want something different from what we have, don't we? The grass is always greener on the other side of the fence. I'd love to have long legs, but I've got used to being tiny. You can get used to anything if you have to.'

They all chatted amicably around the table until the lengthening shadows became swallowed up in the darkness of the night. In the bushes at the edge of the garden, Rebecca could hear the nocturnal sounds of the insects, and for a moment she was transported back to the long hot summers she had spent in this part of Brittany.

'Funny how things tend to go full circle,' she said, half to herself. 'I lived here as a child, and now that I've returned I feel as if I've never been away.'

'You'll fit in admirably,' Dr Sabatier said, giving her an admiring glance. 'That is if Patrick can bear to part with you.'

Rebecca glanced across the table, but the young doctor's eyes were averted. He was giving nothing away, but she had the impression they'd been discussing her relationship with Patrick before she'd arrived at the table.

When Patrick eventually arrived, after his round of the patients, Rebecca noticed how a chair was quickly pushed by her side so that they could sit together.

A discussion of some of the patients followed, Patrick outlining treatments and medication and listening to medical problems put forward by his staff.

The sound of a gong was heard from the interior of La Colombière.

Karine Griffon got to her feet. 'Dinner's ready,' she announced. 'Are you two going to join us?'

'Not tonight,' Patrick said as he stood up. 'I've booked a table at La Fontaine in the village.'

'Oh, very smart,' said Karine, a touch of envy creeping into her voice. 'Well, I hope you enjoy yourselves.'

'We will,' said Patrick, taking hold of Rebecca's arm and leading her away towards his car.

The restaurant was crowded, but the general ambience was one of calm, no hurry, take your time. Rebecca wished she had had time to change after her long day. She was still in the same stone-coloured linen suit she had pulled on at the crack of dawn, and she was feeling a bit crumpled.

But Patrick didn't seem to notice as he smiled down at her and led her through to a corner table. A white-coated waiter handed him the menu and disappeared in search of the bottle of champagne he had ordered.

'What's the celebration?' Rebecca asked, smiling at Patrick across the table.

'The start of a beautiful. . .' he paused, as if searching for the right words.

Rebecca held her breath until he spoke again.

'. . .friendship,' he finished, his eyes searching her face.

She swallowed hard as she met his gaze unflinchingly. If this was friendship, then she wanted more. . .much more! And just for tonight she would forget that other people existed. Only Patrick and herself were real. Time enough to work out the complications later. . .tomorrow. . .or whenever. . .

The bubbles fizzed up her nose as she raised the glass to her lips, and she laughed.

'That's better,' Patrick said with a broad smile. 'I'm glad you've decided to relax. What's that phrase you English have? To let down your hair. . .talking of which. . .'

His hands, moving swiftly across the table, took her by surprise. The long deft fingers unfastened the clasp from the top of her head and her long hair cascaded about her shoulders.

He removed his hand from her hair, but his fingers lingered over hers on the white damask tablecloth. 'Spun gold,' he whispered. 'Why don't you always wear your hair like that?'

Rebecca took another sip of champagne, not wanting the heady moment to evaporate. 'It's not practicable to wear it like this when I'm on duty,' she explained.

'I'm not talking about when you're on duty—that's another world altogether. When we're alone I want you to wear it just like that. . .carefree, so that I can run my hands through it. . .'

'Patrick, this is madness! We can't go on like this,' she began, but his fingers tightened over hers.

'We can live for the moment,' he told her huskily. He took his hand away from hers to adjust the candle-stick in the middle of their table. Gently he moved it to one side so that the flame didn't impede their view of each other. The door to the outer hall opened and the slight draught blew over the candle, causing it to splutter and go out.

A waiter leaned across their table and relighted it, but for a moment Rebecca had felt a chill wind blowing over her, even though the temperature of the res-taurant was summer-hot. She knew she was playing with fire; her fingers would be scorched before the flame went out and she was left to pick up the pieces. But could anything that felt as wonderful as this be wrong?

Don't think about it, she told herself, as she looked across the table at the man who had captivated her heart. She was going to take Patrick's advice and live for the moment.

They had *escargots* for starters, and there was much laughter as Rebecca tried to master the art of removing the garlicky snails from their shells.

'It's years since I tried this,' she smiled. 'My grand-father used to prepare one for me and put it on a piece of bread. But I never had a whole plateful to myself.'

'You've got to get used to *escargots* if you're going to live in France,' Patrick told her. 'You're here for a whole year, you know.'

Their eyes met across the table. 'A lot can happen in a year,' she told him. 'I wish we could look into the future and see what will happen.'

'Better that we take it one day at a time,' he said softly.

After the *escargots*, they had pepper steaks with mushrooms, followed by a salad and some delicious Camembert.

'We'll take coffee on the balcony,' Patrick told the waiter, and led Rebecca between the tables and out through long casement windows to a wide balcony that looked out over the restaurant garden towards a distant view of the sea, illuminated in places by little pinpricks of light from the boats moored near to the shore.

Rebecca could see the rhythmical shafts of light from the lighthouse on the point of the cove, and there were hidden lights in the garden. She felt as if she were part of some giant fairy-tale, totally removed from reality.

'Happy?' murmured Patrick, pulling his chair closer to hers.

'Mm. It's been a wonderful day.' She turned to look at this handsome stranger, this man who had come out of nowhere and turned her world upside down.

'It's not over yet,' he whispered.

She tried to ignore the apprehensive shiver that ran down her spine. Some little part of her was insisting that it couldn't last. . .you couldn't stay this happy forever. . .

'There's a telephone call for you, Dr Delan.'

A waiter had materialised, carrying a portable phone.

Deep down inside, Rebecca instinctively knew this would bring them back to earth. She waited with bated breath as Patrick spoke into the receiver.

'But how serious is her condition?' she heard him say, and her spirits plummeted.

He covered the mouthpiece with his hand as he listened to the reply. 'It's Florence,' he whispered to Rebecca. 'She's been admitted to the Clinique with suspected appendicitis.'

Rebecca's euphoria evaporated. Her professional interest was aroused, but she couldn't help the feeling of anticlimax that swept over her. Why now? Why did Florence have to be ill at this precise moment?

'If we leave now,' Patrick was saying, 'we'll be in Paris in about five hours. The roads will be quiet during the night. You're sure Madame Maurin doesn't require immediate surgery?'

He was listening again before he spoke in reply. 'If her condition worsens, you'd better operate—we can't risk a ruptured appendix and peritonitis. But if she remains stable I'll take over in the morning. Have the theatre staff on standby.'

'So we're going back?' queried Rebecca.

Patrick looked worried as he called for the bill. 'We have no choice. I'd never forgive myself if something happened to Florence. When her husband was dying in hospital, after the crash, I promised him I'd take care of her. And she's asking for me now.'

CHAPTER SEVEN

THE roads were clear of heavy traffic as they drove through the night back to Paris. Rebecca insisted on taking her turn with the driving, knowing how dangerous it would be if one of them were to fall asleep at the wheel. She had never driven an automatic before, but she soon got the hang of it. Although the Peugeot was a big heavy car, it handled like a dream, once she had managed to pull the seat far enough forward so that she could get her feet on the pedals. Patrick stayed awake for her first stint at the wheel, but showed his confidence in her by falling asleep after that.

As the first light of dawn crept over the sleepy city they reached Paris. Rebecca was driving at the time, but she was glad Patrick had remained awake on this last leg of the journey to direct her off the Périphérique at the Pont des Puttes, through the Bois de Boulogne and down the rue Ste-Catherine.

Patrick's second in command, Dr Alain Laval, came hurrying into the foyer as soon as they arrived, his face creased in a frown.

'I really don't know what to make of it, Patrick,' he began. 'The temperature has dropped, but Madame Maurin is obviously in considerable pain. She refused a sedative last night, saying she didn't want any medication until she'd seen you.'

79

Rebecca glanced at Patrick and saw the worry lines on his forehead.

'Better take me to her,' he said tersely. 'Are the theatre staff on the alert?'

'Of course,' the young doctor replied.

As Rebecca followed on behind, she wondered if Patrick would want her on the case. Once she tried to attract his attention, but he was too heavily engrossed in grilling Alain Laval to notice her.

She quickened her pace behind the two men as she realised just how much Florence meant to Patrick. His concern was that of a doctor, but he was obviously deeply involved with her. But she realised that she herself must put away any feelings of animosity towards the woman in Patrick's life. Florence was now a patient in their care. Her very life might depend on their combined skills, and she must forget all the aversion that had been building up.

Florence Maurin was lying in a semi-dark room on the second floor. As Rebecca went through the door she had the impression that their patient was asleep, but the long lashes flew open as Patrick bent over the bed.

'Patrick!. . .oh, Patrick, you came back!' Florence whispered in a thin, wavering voice. Rebecca watched as the long, slender arms slid up around his neck, pulling him closer.

'How are you feeling now, Florence?' Patrick asked gently.

'Awful! The pain is dreadful. I don't know how I've survived the night.'

'We'd better take a look at you.' He seemed to be particularly brisk.

The navy-blue-clad night sister who had been hovering by the bed now stepped forward and rolled back the sheets to a convenient point.

Patrick moved away to scrub his hands in warm water at the sink in the corner of the room. Rebecca stood at the bedside, feeling decidedly redundant. Florence had closed her eyes again and was quietly moaning. Night Sister glanced at Rebecca.

'There is no need for you to stay, Sister Manson,' she said. 'You must be tired after your journey.'

Florence opened her eyes and focused on Rebecca. 'I didn't know you were here,' she whispered. 'Please go back to the house. I left the children with Edith, my maid, but I would prefer you to be there with them.'

For an instant Rebecca hesitated. She was a hospital sister, not a nursemaid! Ever since moving into Florence's *chambre de bonne* she had studiously ignored requests for babysitting. But this was an emergency she would have to cover.

She glanced at Patrick as she left the room, but he was already beginning his examination and seemed to have forgotten her existence.

Outside in the Rue Ste-Catherine the cars stood like sentinels on either side. Everything was Sunday-morning quiet; nothing moved except a couple of elderly ladies walking their pampered pets. The smell of fresh croissants from the *boulangerie* was too inviting to ignore.

Rebecca called in and bought a baguette and four

croissants. Presumably the children and the maid would require breakfast, and she herself was starving.

The concierge greeted her as she went in through the opulent doorway of the apartment block. He had been very helpful when she had moved into her lovely quarters. She told him she was going to go up and help the maid with the Maurin children.

The concierge nodded gravely and asked after Madame Maurin.

'She's being well cared for at the Clinique,' Rebecca told him as they went towards the lift.

The concierge opened the lift gates for her and stood back as he enquired if Madame Maurin would have to have an operation.

'We can't tell at this stage,' Rebecca replied evasively.

Edith, the young maid, opened the door of the apartment, and smiled with relief when she saw Rebecca.

'*Oh, mademoiselle, je suis très contente de vous voir. Les enfants. . .*'

She didn't have to finish her sentence for Rebecca to realise that *les enfants* had been leading the poor maid a dance ever since they'd wakened up. The noise from the kitchen was overpowering.

Rebecca hurried through the kitchen door and, in carefully worded French, asked why they were screaming at each other.

The noise stopped. Olivier and Louise looked at each other and giggled.

'Why do you talk with that funny accent?' seven-year-old Louise asked.

'Because my first language is English. I come from England. Have you ever been there?'

The children looked interested. 'No, we haven't been to England,' eight-year-old Olivier replied. 'How do you get there?'

Rebecca, having got their attention, now started to put the bread and croissants on the kitchen table.

'Help me to set out the breakfast and I'll tell you all about England while we eat,' she said firmly.

The maid had disappeared, but Rebecca was happy to be in total charge of the situation. Children had never been a problem to her and she knew she could cope with whatever came along.

They had a long, leisurely breakfast, while she told stories about England, explaining the different ways of getting there, by air, by sea and even by land, through the Channel tunnel.

They're nice children, she thought as they helped her clear away and restore the kitchen to its pristine condition. It was one of those high-tech rooms, totally aseptic, completely in white, even to the tiles on the floor. It reminded her of Florence's attitude to herself—cold and clinical.

At which point she wondered if she should ring the Clinique and ask after the patient. But she decided against it. Even if Patrick had decided to operate at once the diagnosis wouldn't be clear.

She amused the children until midday, when the maid returned, looking rather guilty at her prolonged absence but explaining that she had had to go home to take care of her boyfriend, having been summoned to take care of her mistress's children at short notice the evening before.

Rebecca made it clear that Edith should have consulted her first.

'Until Madame Maurin returns, I shall be in charge here, Edith,' she explained, in a firm voice. 'That is unless Dr Delan is here, in which case he will give you your instructions.'

Edith replied that she understood and that she would co-operate with *mademoiselle*, but she would require a rise in wages if there was going to be more work thrust upon her.

Rebecca nodded and assured the young woman that she would speak to Dr Delan, but at the moment their main concern was to care for the children in their mother's absence.

The phone rang and Rebecca hurried to pick it up. As she'd hoped, it was Patrick.

'How is she?' she blurted out before he could tell her anything.

There was a pause, several seconds of complete silence at the other end.

'Patrick, what's the matter?' She turned to Edith and told her to take the children to their playroom.

'Is anyone else listening?' Patrick's voice on the phone sounded strained.

'No, we're quite alone now,' she assured him.

'I don't know how to tell you this, but Florence's symptoms were entirely psychosomatic. The pain she claimed to have felt in the right iliac fossa was completely imaginary.'

'But the high temperature? Didn't you say she had a high temperature last night?'

There was a pause. 'Either she worked herself up into a state or else. . .'

'Or else what?'

'Well, I asked the nurse who took her temperature on admission if she'd remained with the patient while the thermometer was in her mouth. She said she'd actually had to slip out of the room for a moment, and. . .'

'But you're not suggesting that Florence did something to the thermometer. . .?' Rebecca's voice trailed away as she remembered playing tricks once when she was a student nurse in sick bay. She'd dipped her thermometer in her cocoa and frightened the night nurse with an impossibly high reading! Yes, it was sometimes done for a joke, but to deliberately falsify the reading. . .and what was the point?

'I think it was a cry for help,' Patrick told her in a sober tone. 'To draw attention to herself. She was probably feeling neglected.'

'Neglected!' Rebecca's eyes scanned the expensive kitchen as she compared Florence's pampered, easy lifestyle with her own hitherto spartan existence. 'Florence seems to have everything in life to make her comfortable,' she blurted out as her own weariness lowered her guard.

'Everything but a man in her life,' came the sobering reply at the other end of the telephone. 'I realise just how much she depends on me. I shouldn't have left her this weekend. She was depressed before I even left. . .she'd even talked about taking her own life. . . Rebecca, are you still there?'

'Yes, I'm still here,' she replied quietly. 'You'd better do what you can to prevent any further hardship in Florence's life. . .and Patrick, we mustn't see each other again except in a professional capacity. I couldn't stand the strain.'

She put the phone down and leaned against the wall, her heart beating madly and her head aching. She put a hand up to her forehead and wiped away the beads of sweat that had formed as she talked to Patrick. She'd told him it was madness to become involved as they had done, and in such a short time.

She moved across the kitchen and sat down at the table. It was a good thing her senses had returned in time to stop her making a fool of herself. Yes, it had been madness. . .but oh, such sweet madness!

The phone rang again. She knew it would be Patrick. . .and she let it ring. . .on. . .and on. . .

CHAPTER EIGHT

IT WAS almost Christmas. The weeks had flown by as Rebecca immersed herself in her medical work at the Clinique. It was a satisfying job, extremely demanding, but one which left her no time to worry about her personal life. . .or rather the lack of it!

As she hurried along the Boulevard Haussmann, her arms aching with the weight of the Christmas presents she had bought in Galeries Lafayette, Prisunic, Marks and Spencer and innumerable other smaller shops, she reflected that she would barely have time to get back to the Clinique for her evening duty. It had been madness to try to achieve all her Christmas shopping in three hours of afternoon off-duty.

And madness was something she was trying to avoid! She was trying to remain sane and sober, concentrating on her work and ignoring the occasional cry from deep within her.

She reached the top of the steps that led down into the Métro at Havre-Caumartin. One hand struggled to hold on to the parcels while the other fished in her coat pocket for her *carnet* of tickets.

One of the parcels slipped from her fingers, and as she stooped wearily to pick it up, a feeling of defiance crept over her. The Métro would be crowded, and much too hot after the freezing cold of the Paris streets. So she would get a cab, and hang the expense! It was

time she gave herself a little treat after the weeks of
frugal saving.

She began to walk, her spirits lifting with the sense
of recklessness. Chris had no right, in his letters, to
urge constant frugality upon her. She was the one who
was making the money, while he was simply concentrating on himself all the time.

She turned occasionally as she walked, to scan the
road for a cab, but they were always occupied. Apart
from the strain on her arms she didn't mind too much.
The air was crisp and early evening frosty, and the
hustle and bustle of the Paris streets was full of the
excitement of Christmas.

She had wandered on to the avenue de l'Opéra, and
still no cab. A tiny pavement café seemed to beckon to
her as she began to walk past. Even in the depths of
winter, people still sat outside in the late afternoon
sun, swathed in thick coats and scarves as they drank
hot coffee or glasses of something stronger.

Rebecca sank down on to one of the chairs, dumping
her parcels on to another one. She would have a coffee
and then telephone to say she was going to be late.
There was nothing urgent on at the Clinique this
evening and she knew that for once they were over-
staffed. They could easily make out until she arrived,
and then she would work longer at the end of her duty.

'Mind if I join you?'

The impeccable English startled her, but not so much
as her recognition of the voice.

'Patrick!' Her voice wavered as she looked up into
the deep blue eyes. 'What are you doing here?'

He smiled, that leisurely, sensual movement of the

lips that had such a devastating effect on her. 'I might ask you the same question.' His eyes danced mischievously. 'I thought you were on duty this evening.'

'I am. . . I've been trying to get a cab and. . .'

'I know. . . I've been following you.' He raised a hand to attract the attention of one of the waiters from inside. '*Deux Ricards, s'il vous plaît.*'

She attempted to rise, reaching for her parcels. 'I really should be getting back and. . .'

His firm hand on her arm detained her. 'So should I. We'll go together. My car is just around the corner— I've been doing some Christmas shopping. When I saw you striding out I was intrigued. I decided to try and park so that I could offer you a lift. I knew it would be no good simply stopping beside you in the street, you'd simply have walked on.'

The colour rose to her cheeks as she turned to face him. She was planning what she should say, but she hesitated until the waiter had put their drinks on the table and retreated back into the steamy warmth of the café.

'Patrick, I'm sorry if I've avoided you since. . .since Brittany, but we both know it's the only way out of the dilemma. I mean, Chris's leg has been more complicated than we anticipated, and Florence has shown she's perfectly capable of committing suicide, or at least pretending to, and. . .'

'And here we both are, caught in the middle of it,' he said in a resigned tone as he poured water into their glasses of Ricard from a stone pitcher. The liquid clouded over as he raised his glass towards her. 'We don't deserve our fate, do we?'

Rebecca lifted her glass as her eyes met his. It was the first time since their idyllic weekend in Brittany that she had dared to look him straight in the eye. In fact, it was the first time they had been alone. . .if you could call it being alone, surrounded as they were by crowds of shoppers, hurrying past and bumping against their table.

'Please don't say it, Patrick. I've tried so hard to. . .'

'You've tried so hard to avoid me, Rebecca. You've been super-efficient and coldly clinical when we've had to work together.'

'And you've been bossy, demanding, critical, arrogant. . .the staff think you dislike me. Jacqueline told me the other day not to take you too seriously. She said that underneath all your strict discipline you were an extremely likeable man. She said that your personality in the Clinique——'

'She should have said that underneath I was concealing all my feelings for you,' he interposed heatedly. 'That when a situation is hopeless you have to cut off the life-support system. It's no good keeping alive false hopes.'

'Yours or mine?' she whispered.

His hand reached across the table and took hold of hers. 'Both,' he murmured as his fingers enclosed hers.

'Then we're both acting out a part, aren't we?' she said quietly.

He nodded. 'And so is Florence. Every time she has one of her panic attacks or gets depressed she invents an ailment to get my sympathy. I actually caught her reading through one of her husband's medical text-books, so I'm not sure what I'm in for next!'

Rebecca smiled. 'You're very philosophical, Patrick.'

Patrick gave a wry grin. 'It's the only way. Florence was an actress before she married a doctor, so the combination of the acting profession and a basic knowledge of medicine can be positively dangerous. Sometimes I don't know why I put up with it.'

'Yes, I've often wondered that,' she said, in a bland tone. 'What will Florence have to do before you desert her?'

He hesitated as if searching for the right words. 'I'm not sure. I promised her husband Michel I would look after her. I'm hoping against hope that. . .'

She waited, holding her breath, for him to continue, but his eyes held a veiled expression.

'Hoping against hope that what?' she prompted.

He shook his head. 'No, you must forget I started to say that. I have to take care of her until. . .until she doesn't need me any more. And in the meantime——'

'But she'll always need you,' Rebecca blurted out passionately. 'Just as Chris needs me. There's no resolution to the problem. We're both caring people, trained to look after the medical needs of others. . .to put ourselves last. So we have to be realistic. . .oh, why did you follow me here today? Why couldn't you have left things as they were?'

He reached across the table and took both her hands in his, gazing adoringly into her eyes. Her cold hands warmed at his touch and a shiver of excitement ran through her.

'I followed you today because I was worried about you. Because you're only half the girl you were when we first met. You've lost your *joie de vivre*, the spring in your step. . .and I feel responsible for making you unhappy. Please let me make it up to you. Let me take you out of yourself. An evening out in pre-Christmas Paris would bring the colour back to your cheeks. I promise we would be just good friends enjoying a night on the town. What do you say?'

She opened her mouth to quash the idea before it could take further shape. But the look in his eyes made her legs turn to jelly. That indefinable liquid feeling that was coursing through her body demolished all her hard resolve.

'You make it sound so inviting,' she said, half to herself.

Her voice was drowned in the noise of the traffic.

Patrick squeezed her hands. 'You'll have to speak up. Was that a yes or a no?'

She smiled. 'Who was it that said he could resist everything but temptation? Was it Oscar Wilde?'

He laughed, a deep, resonant, sensual sound that made the people on the next table smile to see the happiness of the couple, so obviously in love. 'I don't care who said it first, so long as you say it now. Look in your diary, Rebecca. How about tomorrow evening?'

Now it was her turn to laugh. 'I don't have to look in my diary to give you an answer. My social engage-ments are non-existent, but I do know I'm on duty tomorrow evening.'

'Change it. You're in charge of the obstetrics unit now, and I know for a fact that you're over-staffed. I made sure we appointed enough trained nurses so that you wouldn't find the work too exhausting. I couldn't run the risk of having you leave the Clinique.'

Rebecca swallowed hard, as she gazed deep into his eyes. It had never been like this with Chris. There had never been such a feeling of sensual euphoria. Sitting here, in this cold street, she felt summer-hot. The darkening sky appeared blue and cloudless to her. The noise of the traffic was the sound of the waves beating against the shore of a tropical island where she and Patrick were totally alone together.

She spoke slowly, carefully to conceal her true feelings. 'I would enjoy an evening out with you, Patrick. . .so long as we were just good friends.'

A mischievous smile played on his lips as he said, 'But of course. I shall be perfectly correct towards you, *mademoiselle*. And I shall return my Cinderella to her home before the stroke of midnight, lest her carriage turn into a pumpkin.'

Rebecca giggled, feeling relieved that the tension had been broken. She reached for her parcels, but Patrick was already there, gathering them up into his strong arms. As she stood up, he reached down, in full view of the intrigued onlookers, and kissed her lightly on the cheek, before exhorting her to hang on to his arm.

They battled their way through the rush-hour crowds back to Patrick's car. As he opened the passenger door for her, she suddenly remembered she hadn't phoned the Clinique.

'No problem,' he told her. 'You can use my car phone. Everything was quiet when I left a couple of hours ago, and we're overstaffed tonight.'

'I know. That was why I decided to slow down and
take the weight off my legs. I was exhausted before
you came along.'

'You've perked up considerably,' he said as he
stretched his long legs inside the car. 'Must have been
the Ricard.'

Their eyes met, but neither of them spoke.

Rebecca was an hour late on duty, but none of the staff
on the obstetrics unit commented on the fact. Brigitte
Taralon, the junior sister, had been perfectly happy to
assume control. She was newly appointed at the
Clinique, having returned to nursing after the birth of
her baby daughter. Her husband was out of work, so her
mother was looking after the little girl so that Brigitte
could earn some much-needed cash. When Rebecca had
spoken to her from Patrick's car, Brigitte had told her
not to hurry back; everything was under control.

The private rooms were all quiet as Rebecca did her
evening round. Only the occasional crying of one of
the new infants disturbed the peace.

It's been like this for a couple of days now, she
reflected. There were two empty rooms, prepared for
a couple of mothers-to-be who were due in a few days'
time, but otherwise there had been no deliveries. She
stopped longer than was necessary with each of her
new mothers, listening to their problems, helping them
with feeding, advising when they should go home and
generally creating a feeling of calm that would help
them sleep more easily.

She found herself smiling a great deal, even laughing
with the patients who joked with her. And all the time

she hugged against herself the deep, deep secret of her meeting with Patrick and the magical transformation just being with him had made.

As she sat at her desk, writing out a report for the night staff, Brigitte Taralon came into the office. Rebecca looked up.

'It's time you were going, Brigitte. I'll stay on for a while. . .oh, but there's just one thing. Would you like to work an extra evening this week. . .say tomorrow?'

The young blonde-haired sister smiled. 'Yes, of course. I'm always happy to do extra hours. And we've gone to live in my mother's apartment now, so there's no problem with babysitting.' She turned at the door. 'Are you going somewhere exciting, Sister?'

Rebecca smiled, unable to disguise the happiness she felt. 'I expect so.'

CHAPTER NINE

THE theatre of the Comédie Française was smaller than Rebecca had imagined it would be. All her life she had longed to go and see the famous theatre company, but in her mind's eye she had envisaged the surroundings as something like the Royal Albert Hall. Glancing around now from her seat in the orchestra stalls, she decided that she approved of the cosy, intimate feeling the theatre gave her. And the plush old-fashioned seats and ornate carving on the boxes induced an ambience of a bygone, more leisurely era.

Patrick leaned across and handed her a programme. 'I hope you like the writing of Victor Hugo. I've actually seen this play, *Marie Tudor*, before, but I thought you would enjoy it as it's supposed to take place in London. The costumes and the setting are simply spectacular.'

She gave a whimsical smile. 'I hope it won't make me homesick!'

'Do you think it might?' he asked in a pseudo-serious voice, with only a hint of laughter dancing in his deep blue eyes.

She shook her head vigorously. 'No chance!'

As the lights began to dim, he took hold of her hand. 'We're just good friends, remember,' he whispered into her ear.

'Don't worry, I hadn't forgotten, but I thought you might have,' she replied under her breath.

He squeezed her hand but didn't answer. The curtain rose, and Rebecca felt the vibrant enthusiasm of the cast reaching out to claim her attention.

She was enthralled throughout the whole of the performance. It was a good three hours before the final curtain went down amid cheers and clapping. Patrick released her hand as they moved into the crowded foyer. They were hemmed in by enthusiastic Parisians, laughing, gesticulating with their hands, excitedly discussing the play.

It had been like this during the interval, when they had fought their way through to drink champagne at the busy little bar. But the crush couldn't dampen Rebecca's happiness. Three whole hours beside Patrick had seemed like a lifetime in one respect, and in another it had whisked past too quickly.

She felt his arm protecting her back as she moved slowly forward towards the fresh air streaming in from the rue de Richelieu. Minutes later they were outside, breathing in the cold air, which seemed like wine after the claustrophobic foyer.

'That's better,' said Patrick as he held up his hand to attract the attention of one of the waiting taxis. 'It's a good thing I ordered our cab in advance.'

He helped her into the back seat before asking what she thought of the show.

'Original in its approach,' Rebecca replied. 'It wasn't at all as I imagined Victor Hugo would have intended it to be. . .and I don't think Mary Tudor was at all as she was portrayed. But from an entertainment point of view I thought it was fantastic.'

He smiled as he pulled her against his side, leaning back against the seat. 'You obviously love going to the theatre. We'll have to go again together. It's something that friends can do, you know.'

She laughed. 'Well, I'm glad we've found the perfect recreation for us.'

'Oh, yes; theatregoing is perfectly harmless. It doesn't lead anywhere. . .except on to one of my favourite restaurants for dinner.'

Rebecca suppressed the shiver of excitement that ran through her as she listened to Patrick giving directions to the taxi driver. They were leaving the Rive Droite, crossing the Seine, shimmering with numerous lights from the *bateaux mouches*, and heading for the Quartier Latin. She caught a glimpse of Notre-Dame, bathed in a magnificent, kaleidoscopic glow of illumination, before the taxi whisked them along the Boulevard St-Michel, turning off with a screech of tyres into a maze of narrow, cobbled streets.

As Patrick paid the driver, requesting him to return in a couple of hours, Rebecca looked up at the intriguing façade of the restaurant. From the outside, it had the appearance of a tiny street house, but it opened out on the inside into a well-appointed set of rooms. The first, being the welcoming area, was complete with a tiny bar. As the waiter took their order, they sat by the window, drinking more champagne and watching the Parisian night-life. Couples wandered past their window, arms entwined, eyes shining with excitement as they gazed at each other.

Patrick reached for her hand. 'Happy?' he whispered.

She smiled up into his eyes. 'Need you ask?'

They sat in contented silence until their table was ready. It had a red and white check tablecloth, a single long-stemmed rose in the centre and a candle that dripped wax into a porcelain bowl of rose-petals. Somewhere in the background a young man was playing an accordion.

'I used to come here when I was a medical student,' Patrick told Rebecca. 'It's my kind of place. It used to be very cheap until the smart set found it and everyone wanted to come. The prices went up accordingly, but it hasn't lost its old charm.'

Plates of succulent *foie gras* arrived, followed by a *cassoulet*. The music became louder and more insistent as their meal progressed. Patrick pulled Rebecca to her feet and spun her around the tiny dancing area. She had a feeling of unreality as if she were in a dream. And it was a dream that she wanted to go on forever and ever. She didn't want to wake up and find herself alone, without Patrick.

They lingered over their coffee after a deliciously melt-in-your-mouth *crème caramel*. There was a plate of tiny *petits fours* in the middle of their table, but Rebecca said she couldn't be tempted to another morsel.

'A delicious meal, Patrick. I'm glad you persuaded me to come out tonight.'

His eyes held a tender expression. 'So am I. You look more like the girl I . . .' He stopped, his mouth moving into a casual smile before he continued, 'The girl I fell in love with, and——'

'Please, Patrick, don't say things like that!'

He eyed her mischievously. 'I wish you wouldn't interrupt. I was going on to say that after falling in love with you I have now made you my best friend. Now there's nothing wrong in that, is there?'

She gave him a wry grin. 'Patrick Delan, you're impossible. I give up!'

He opened his eyes in wide exaggeration. 'Do you mean you give in?'

She laughed. 'You know perfectly well what I mean.'

A waiter leaned across to tell them that their taxi was waiting outside.

Patrick went round to hold the back of Rebecca's chair as she stood up. 'Just time for a nightcap at my place, I think,' he whispered in a voice that sent shivers of anticipation down her spine.

They went out into the freezing cold of the small hours. Some of the earlier frenetic frivolity was absent from the streets, but there was still a lot of activity.

As the taxi whisked them back to the sixteenth arrondissement, Rebecca allowed herself to revel in being close to Patrick on the back seat. His arm lay loosely around her shoulders and she wanted these few precious minutes to go on forever.

'I've asked the driver to take us back to the Clinique,' Patrick told her. 'I promised Night Sister I'd look in on my post-operative patients, however late it happened to be. Alain Laval is perfectly capable, but, at the end of the day, they're my responsibility. It'll only take me a few minutes, so if you wait in the foyer we can walk round to the apartment.'

'Do you need any help?' she asked.

He smiled into her eyes. 'No, thanks. Night Sister Souzan would feel you were encroaching on her territory.'

Rebecca gave a wry grin. 'Blanche Souzan would also take a delight in telling Florence—I believe they get on well together.'

Patrick's eyes held a defiant look. 'I don't mind what Florence hears about us. She can think what she likes.'

Rebecca sighed. 'But are you willing to pick up the pieces? Are you ready to cope with another emotional display, a violent tantrum, a suicidal threat?'

His arms tightened around her, and she felt his hot breath fanning her face as he leaned very close. 'One day, my love, we'll be free. Trust me.'

When his lips claimed hers she felt liquid desire running through her. She longed to abandon herself to his caresses and she welcomed his long, lingering kiss.

When he drew away, their eyes remained locked in a secret understanding. Rebecca knew they would always love each other, no matter what happened. Their love had been made in heaven, and it was indestructible.

Patrick helped her out of the cab, paid the driver, and followed her up the wide stone steps of the Clinique. She kept herself deliberately apart from him as they went into the foyer. The blonde night receptionist looked up from the book she was reading at the desk and smiled as she enquired how she could help *monsieur le docteur*.

'Sister Souzan is expecting me,' Patrick told her. 'I'm going up to the surgical unit to check on the patients I operated on today, or rather yesterday.'

'Very good, sir, but first would you mind taking a look at the newly admitted patient? He arrived just before midnight and he's been asking especially to see you. . .and Sister Manson.' The receptionist broke off and looked at Rebecca. 'I believe he's a close friend of yours, *mademoiselle*. His name is Christopher Preston.'

'Chris? Chris is here in Paris? But he's not due out until the New Year. There was a problem with his leg and——'

'Excuse me, Sister,' the receptionist interrupted, 'I believe the young man decided to come out here against medical advice. I've already contacted the London hospital where he was receiving treatment and they have assured me that Christopher Preston signed himself out.'

Rebecca's face was grim as she enquired which room Chris had been given.

The corridor was deathly quiet as she hurried along, trying to keep up with Patrick's long strides. So far, he had refrained from making any comment on Chris's untimely arrival. Inside, Rebecca was fuming. It was just like Chris to take the law into his own hands. It wasn't the first time that his headstrong, impulsive behaviour had landed him in trouble. He surely could have waited until the New Year, especially after the complications to his fractured femur.

Patrick pushed open the door of Chris's private room and Rebecca went in. Chris was lying on top of the bed, fully clothed, smoking a cigarette.

'Please don't smoke in here,' Rebecca told him quietly.

Chris pulled himself up against the head of the bed. 'Well, that's a nice welcome, I must say! I travel all the way over from London and this is how you greet me. You could at least say you're pleased to see me.'

Rebecca's eyes scanned the room, taking in the crutches placed strategically by the bed and the wheelchair over by the window.

'How did you get here from London?'

'I swam the Channel, of course,' Chris replied, in a belligerent tone, as he blew a smoke-ring towards the ceiling.

Patrick stepped forward and held out his hand. 'I'm Dr Patrick Delan. You will be initially in my care until we can assess what treatment you are to receive in our convalescent home.'

For a moment the young man looked puzzled as he accepted the welcoming hand and shook it before leaning his blond head back against the pillows. 'So you're not mad at me for coming out early, Doc?'

Patrick hesitated. 'I'm sure it was most inconvenient for the hospital in London to have you sign yourself out, but we'll have to make the best of it. Now, perhaps you would tell me how you made the journey over here.'

Some of the wind had gone out of Chris's sails as he began his explanation. 'I just couldn't stand hanging around any longer, so I rang up Heathrow and booked myself on an Air France flight. I told them I was on crutches, so they met me at the airport with a wheelchair. Same thing happened this end at Charles de

Gaulle as well. They put me into a taxi. I didn't have
any French money, but I told the man to call back here
in the morning and my fiancée would pay.' He grinned.
'I told him I wasn't going anywhere after I'd checked
into this hospital!'

Rebecca turned as she heard the door opening. Night
Sister Blanche Souzan was a formidable lady, totally
dedicated to her work of the past twenty years and
brooking no indiscipline either from her staff or her
patients.

'I thought I told you to get undressed, young man,'
she began in rapid French, as she bore down upon the
hapless Chris, reaching for the buttons of his shirt.

Chris had no problem with French, this being the
subject he taught in language schools, and the tone of
the large, bossy lady did not intimidate him.

'OK, OK, keep your hair on, dear! I was going to
get undressed when I'd finished my cigarette, so. . .'

Sister Souzan released her grip on Chris's shirt,
wrenched the cigarette from his fingers and hurled it
into the sink. 'Smoking is strictly forbidden,' she said
firmly. It was only after this display of her obvious
disapproval that she turned to address Rebecca. 'Perhaps you could persuade your friend to undress so that
Dr Delan can examine him?'

'That won't be necessary,' Patrick put in. 'Mr
Preston will get a full examination and assessment in
the morning. The most important thing is for him to
settle into his room and go to sleep. Sister Manson is
off duty, so it would be unprofessional if I were to
allow her to remain in this young man's room in the

middle of the night. You have a male nurse on duty, I take it, Sister Souzan?'

The night sister pursed her lips in disapproval of this countermanding of her authority, but she nodded and agreed to send the male nurse along.

After she had gone out, Patrick stood for a moment looking down at Chris. Rebecca surmised he was wondering what she had ever seen in him. At this precise moment, after Chris's display of bad manners, she couldn't remember what it was that had first captured her interest. It was all so long ago. . .way back in their childhood. But he was different then. Now he was a twenty-five-year-old, and somewhere along the way during his school and university education he had picked up some annoying habits and could be thoroughly obnoxious if he chose.

She looked at the florid face that had filled out until she could only describe it as pudgy. Months of inactivity had given his body a puffy appearance. Oh, it was true she felt sorry for him; it couldn't be any fun being incarcerated in hospital with a fractured femur. But he had no need to take it out on other people in this inconsiderate way. Lots of patients were infinitely more incapacitated than he was and they didn't become belligerent.

And as she stood beside Patrick, looking down at the once-loved face, she came to a decision. She would have to tell Chris she no longer loved him. If he was strong enough to travel around by himself like this, he was strong enough to hear the truth. She couldn't go on living a lie. . .but not tonight. She couldn't tell him

tonight. That would be too cruel. . .and she hadn't
thought out what she was going to say.

Gently she patted Chris's hand in an impersonal
way, as she often did when trying to comfort a patient.
'I'll call in to see you in the morning. Sleep well, Chris,'
she said quietly, and, turning away decisively, she left
him alone with Patrick.

It was nearly half an hour later in the foyer before
Patrick caught up with her. She was standing by the
revolving door, staring out at the dark sky, her heart
beating rapidly as she contemplated how she was going
to tell Chris.

She turned at the sound of Patrick's feet crossing the
foyer. His face was uncharacteristically grim as he put
out his hand to push the door. Outside in the cold night
air Rebecca felt a chill around her heart. The mood
had changed. They were no longer enjoying a night on
the town.

He took her arm as he led her down the rue Ste-
Catherine, but there was no tenderness in the gesture.
He was simply being polite and chilvalrous to a lady on
a dark street.

As they reached the apartment block he spoke in a
strangely subdued voice. 'I hadn't realised just how
much your fiancé depends on you or how much he
means to you. I can see why he had to come out here
at this particular time.'

She turned to face him in the half-light as he pressed
the code selector beside the door. He looked so
different from the carefree man who had taken her to
the theatre, wined and dined her and flirted deliciously
so that she had felt like a young girl again.

The door opened; he stood for a moment looking down at her with a sad expression. 'You were right to remain faithful to your fiancé. I would never have forgiven myself if I'd broken up such a strong love-affair.'

'Patrick, you don't understand,' she began, as he escorted her through the door.

'Ah, but I do understand now,' he interposed quickly. 'I had a little chat with Chris and he explained the situation. I'm sorry if you've found my advances unwelcome. I assure you it was only because. . .because I didn't really believe you were in love with your fiancé.'

They had reached the lift. Rebecca stared up into Patrick's serious face. 'What did Chris say to you?' she whispered hoarsely.

A sad smile crossed Patrick's lips. 'I promised not to repeat Chris's confidences to anyone, and especially not to you, Rebecca.'

CHAPTER TEN

REBECCA was awakened by the sound of someone pounding his or her fists on her door. It took several seconds before she could pull her thoughts together, having barely slept through what remained of the hours before dawn. Her head ached from struggling to come to terms with the new situation. Chris had come over from London and had told Patrick something that had changed his whole attitude towards her. Throughout the time that she had tossed sleeplessly in her bed she had asked herself whatever Chris could be up to.

Wearily she reached for her robe. The pounding on the door had begun again, and she recognised the frightened voice of Florence's maid, Edith.

'*Mademoiselle, vous êtes là?*'

'*Oui, j'arrive,*' Rebecca called, as she crossed the tiny *chambre de bonne* and flung open the door.

'*Oh, mademoiselle.*' Edith grasped Rebecca by the arm and tried to pull her out of the room. '*Venez vite! C'est Madame Maurin.*'

Rebecca sighed. 'And just what has your mistress been up to now?'

'*Elle est morte,*' came the chilling reply.

Rebecca's stomach lurched. No, it was impossible. Florence couldn't be dead. It had to be another act, another attempt to get sympathy from Patrick.

'You must fetch Dr Delan,' she told the maid.

108

'*Monsieur le docteur est déjà là.* He is there already,'
Edith told her. 'He told me to bring you to him.'

Rebecca felt a cold numbness around her heart as
she hurried after the maid, her bare feet noiseless on
the carpet of the foyer. As she knotted her cotton robe
tightly around her on their way to the first floor, she
found herself praying that Edith would be mistaken,
that her mistress would still be alive. However she
might have despised Florence, her instinct to preserve
life was too strong to deny.

Patrick's face was ashen as he leaned over the bed in
Florence's sumptuous bedroom. Rebecca noticed that
he was fully dressed in a dark suit, looking as if he was
on his way out to the Clinique. But it was the inert
figure beneath the silken counterpane that captured all
her attention. Florence's white face was painted over
with flawless make-up. Even the lips had been defined
in an immaculate crimson curve. The ivory skin of her
bare shoulders, crossed only by narrow straps of black
silk, seemed only to redefine the awful truth. Florence
had finally taken her own life. . .and yet there was
something that didn't quite fit the usual pat-
tern. . .something that disturbed Rebecca about this
grotesque scenario.

Patrick turned to her, his eyes hollow with anxiety.
'I can detect a feeble pulse. Help me give her a gastric
lavage—there's a tube in my bag.'

'Thank God she's still alive!' Rebecca said as she
began to set up the equipment. 'But how do you know
that she's swallowed something?'

'Because this empty bottle was by the bed this
morning,' Edith interposed excitedly.

Patrick reached out his hand. 'I'll take that, if you don't mind, Edith.' He slipped the bottle into his suit pocket. 'Please go and see to the children. I can hear them waking up; they mustn't come in here. Be quick, get them dressed, give them breakfast, call a cab and take them to school. Tell them their mother is still asleep and must not be disturbed.'

Together they raised the inert figure to a sitting position. Patrick began to pass the tube into Florence's mouth and Rebecca stood by ready to administer the saline.

It was an unpleasant procedure. Rebecca had always disliked giving gastric lavages, but in this particular case it was a life-saving situation.

A couple of hours later Florence had been resuscitated enough to reach up weakly with her thin arms and stroke Patrick's cheek.

'What happened?' she asked, in a feeble voice.

Patrick patted her hand gently. 'You've had a gastric problem, but you're all right now. It must have been something you ate that disagreed with you.' He turned to Rebecca and whispered, 'Thank you so much for your help. I preferred to treat Florence here rather than at the Clinique. You know what it would be like if this story got out, so let's keep it to ourselves. Would you mind staying here for the morning until I get back? I have an important meeting that I must attend. I'll get Sister Taralon to take over in Obstetrics until you arrive.'

'Why are you whispering? Please don't leave me, Patrick,' Florence wailed plaintively.

'Rebecca will take care of you, Florence. I'll be back this afternoon.'

As Rebecca watched the departing figure she reflected fleetingly that it was only hours since she and Patrick had been together in the Left Bank restaurant. Life had been full of promise, exciting, exhilarating. . .and now everything had changed. Florence stood between them again, and Chris was here, spinning some yarn to prolong their relationship.

Well, Florence would be pleased about that! Maybe she would stop making suicide attempts now that Patrick was all hers again.

As she was settling Florence into clean sheets Edith asked if Rebecca would like some coffee. Rebecca said she would but she would come along to the kitchen for it. The time spent in Florence's room had been wearying and she needed a break. Florence would be safe by herself for a few minutes.

The high-tech kitchen was gleaming after Edith's early-morning labours. Rebecca took a sip of the strong black coffee and motioned to Edith to sit down opposite her at the kitchen table.

'Tell me, when did you first realise there was something wrong with your mistress?' she began carefully.

Edith hesitated before replying. 'It was when I heard her private phone ringing and ringing. I knew she should have heard it if she was in her room, so I got up and went along to see her. She was lying in the bed, completely still and lifeless.' The maid's voice quivered. 'Oh, *mademoiselle*, I was sure she was dead. The phone was still ringing, so I picked it up, and it was Dr

Delan asking for *madame*. I told him to come quickly. When he arrived he sent me to fetch you.'

Rebecca frowned. 'Was your mistress unduly disturbed last night?'

Again the maid hesitated and kept her eyes deliberately downcast. '*Madame* doesn't like the doctor to go out. . .with someone else.'

'But was she in the habit of taking sedatives to help her sleep?' Rebecca asked gently.

'Sometimes she would. But Dr Delan had prescribed these new ones for *madame* only a couple of days ago when she was distressed about something. That's why she had a full bottle.'

There was still something that Rebecca had to ask before she could calm her suspicions. She couldn't help remembering that when she'd performed the gastric lavage there had been food mixed with the tablets that Florence had swallowed. It was very unusual for suicide patients to take food in their final attempt at ending it all. On the other hand, if someone else. . .

'Tell me, Edith, did your mistress have a late supper last night?'

The maid's eyes were wide with fright. 'Dr Delan called in, on his way back from. . .wherever he went last night. I heard him chatting to *madame* in the kitchen, and this morning I washed up some coffee-cups and two plates with the remains of a special dessert Madame had prepared.'

Rebecca swallowed hard. So the tablets could have been mixed in with the dessert. But Florence would hardly prepare a dessert and then deliberately poison

herself. . .but it was just possible. . .oh, no! The
alternative was too horrible to contemplate.

Even as the thoughts dashed through her mind she
began to remember Patrick's words as they sat together
at the pavement café in the rue de l'Opéra. He had
sworn to take care of Florence until. . . Rebecca
remembered Patrick had refused to finish the sentence
or explain himself. And she also remembered his words
in the cab last night. 'One day. . .we'll be free. Trust
me. . .'

She stood up from the kitchen table, every nerve-
ending in her body taut and tense. She had to put this
senseless speculation away from her mind. Patrick was
a wonderful man, a man devoted to the care of his
patients. A man whom she loved and wanted. . .even
though he was totally inaccessible. How could she
doubt him?

Patrick returned at noon to relieve Rebecca's watch
on Florence, bringing with him a private nurse.

The young woman wasn't from the Clinique. Patrick
introduced her as Diane Poitiers, an agency nurse who
was temporarily employed to care for Madame Maurin
after her recent attack of gastro-enteritis.

Rebecca's eyes met Patrick's as she heard him pro-
nounce the fictitious diagnosis. His expression was
enigmatic, but she surmised he was daring her to
contradict. She turned away, disliking the subterfuge
but unwilling to be disloyal. If this was what Patrick
wanted then so be it.

Edith announced that she had prepared lunch.
Patrick told her to serve it in the kitchen. . .but nothing

for *madame*. She must rest her digestive system for a few hours.

Rebecca sat down at the kitchen table with Patrick on her right and the new nurse on her left. Edith, somewhat put out by this unusual situation, endeavoured to run between stove and table as she served up *poulet grandmère* from a large earthenware casserole.

Rebecca's appetite was non-existent, but she made a show of eating something to please Edith and make Patrick think she had accepted the events of the past few hours, taking them in her stride. For the first time since meeting Patrick she wanted to get away from him, to be alone with her own thoughts, to try to sort out what it all meant, this macabre charade.

She excused herself as Edith came to the dessert stage and offered them fresh fruit.

'I really must be getting back to the Clinique,' she said abruptly, as she pushed back her chair.

Patrick was on his feet before her. 'So must I. Thank you, Edith. Please give every assistance to Nurse Poitiers, and telephone me at the Clinique if you're worried about your mistress. I'll call in this evening.'

Rebecca walked silently beside Patrick up the rue Ste-Catherine. She wanted no part of the scenario he was enacting. Whatever he was up to, she didn't want to know. She preferred to remember the idyllic times they had spent together before everything changed. Somehow she would have to put all this behind her now.

They had reached the steps of the Clinique before Patrick spoke in a dark, sombre tone.

'Thank you for all your help with Florence, Rebecca. I couldn't have managed without you this morning.'

She paused at the foot of the stairs, suddenly aroused to her normal character from the apathy induced by the strange turn of events. 'Oh, but I think you could,' she said in a firm tone. 'I don't think you needed me at all. I'm not sure what's going on, but I'd rather not be a part of it, Patrick. I don't like living a lie.'

He moved swiftly to take hold of her shoulders, his eyes piercing into her with an intensity she had never seen before.

'This is no lie, Rebecca,' he told her softly. 'But we have to protect Florence's children. Trust me.'

She turned away her head so that he couldn't see her sad expression. 'You told me to trust you last night in the cab. I didn't know how far that trust would be stretched.'

His fingers were under her chin, turning her head so that she was forced to look up into his eyes. 'I don't know what you're implying, Rebecca, but do you honestly think I wanted Florence to make another attempt at suicide?'

She wanted to drown in the expression of tenderness in his eyes. But somewhere deep inside her a little nagging voice was telling her to hold back. How well did she know this man who had swept her off her feet? How long had she known him?. . . A mere three months or so. She had to start thinking with her head and not her heart.

'I don't know what to think,' she murmured. 'But I have to go back on duty. Work is the only thing I understand at the moment.'

She heard his deep sigh as he relinquished his hold on her, and it sounded like the death knell to their relationship. It was over between them. She could feel the awful truth dogging her leaden footsteps as she forced herself to climb the Clinique steps.

She was busy in Obstetrics for a couple of hours before she could find the time to go down to see Chris. There had been a message left on her desk, asking her to see him, but she had studiously ignored this until she had organised her department. She had made it a rule to put patients before personal life when she was on duty. But as she ran lightly down the steps towards Orthopaedics she knew she had been glad of the excuse to prolong her procrastination.

Now just what was she going to tell Chris?

She found him sitting in a chair in his room, staring moodily out of the window.

'And about time too!' he greeted her. 'I'd begun to think you'd run away with Dr Patrick. You do fancy him, don't you? It stuck out a mile when the two of you came in last night. But I soon put him right, warned him off.'

'Chris, what exactly did you tell him?' Rebecca asked evenly, as she crossed to the window and stood looking down at him.

Chris grinned. 'Wouldn't you like to know?'

She sat down on the window-seat, her eyes averted, looking down into the busy street. She knew from past experience that Chris wouldn't tell her any more than he wanted to. She wouldn't be able to worm the truth out of him until he was good and ready.

'We've got to talk, Chris,' she began firmly. 'For

some time now my feelings for you have been changing.'

'That's been pretty obvious,' he interjected harshly. 'You were about to break off our engagement when I fell and broke my leg, weren't you?'

'Was it that obvious?' she asked quietly. 'I didn't want——'

He gave a harsh, mirthless laugh. 'You didn't want me to know you wanted to break things up. You took pity on me when I was in hospital, didn't you?'

'Well, I wouldn't like to put it quite like that. I prefer——'

'Well, how would you like to put it?' he shouted.

The door opened, and Rebecca turned in alarm, to see Patrick standing on the threshold.

'I'm sorry to intrude. I should have knocked, but I heard raised voices and I thought maybe one of the nurses was having a problem.'

'You mean having a problem with your problem patient,' Chris said angrily. 'Go on, tell her, tell my precious ex-fiancée what they said about me in London.'

Rebecca frowned. 'If there's something I should know, I'd like to hear it.'

Patrick closed the door and walked over to the window. He stood looking gravely down at Chris. 'Would you like me to tell Rebecca, Chris?'

The young man shrugged his shoulders. 'Why not? I expect everyone in the hospital knows by now.'

'No, they don't; my phone call to London was highly confidential and made purely for medical reasons, so that we can give you the best treatment,' Patrick interposed quickly. He took a deep breath before turning towards Rebecca. 'It appears that the complications that Chris was suffering before he came out to Paris were not orthopaedic, they were medical.'

A chill ran through Rebecca. 'What do you mean, medical, Patrick?'

'I'll tell you!' Chris shouted, in a voice full of false bravado. 'I'm a junkie!'

'You're nothing of the kind,' Patrick said firmly. 'You happened to be visited in hospital by the wrong kind of friends just when you were feeling run down. You discharged yourself so that you could spend some time with these so-called friends who had offered to look after you, and before you knew where you were you were hooked on drugs and didn't know how to cope.'

'Chris, is this true?'

For once, Chris seemed at a loss for words. He frowned, reached into his pocket and pulled out a cigarette packet. Finding it empty, he crumpled it in disgust and hurled it at the wall. Finally he spoke in a small, almost childlike voice.

'Afraid so. It was that crowd I went out with in my final year at university. Most of them are unemployed, so they had the time to come and visit me. When the orthopaedic consultant said I could go off to a convalescent home in north London for physiotherapy, I asked if I could be a day patient, and he agreed. My pals found room for me in their flat, and that was when the drugs thing started. They knew I had some money saved up, so I was very welcome. I'd smoked cannabis with them when we were students, but I thought it was pretty harmless.'

'I warned you about the dangers,' Rebecca put in. 'You knew you'd start to want something stronger if you kept on like that.'

'I went on to heroin,' Chris said, in a neutral tone. 'After a couple of weeks I stopped going to physiotherapy altogether. That was when they sent someone round to check up on me and persuaded me to go back into hospital. By that time I was glad to get away from my pals, because I was broke.'

'Oh, Chris!' Rebecca shook her head. 'What did the hospital do about it?'

'They tried to keep me off the drugs, of course. I coped for a couple of days. Then my aunt came to see me and I persuaded her to lend me some money so I could come out to see you. She always liked you and she thinks you're a good influence on me.' He gave a weak grin. 'Anyway, I signed myself out, and on the way to the airport I bought a fix from a bloke at Piccadilly Circus. I'm going to need another one soon, and——'

'No, Chris, we've got to kick this thing,' Rebecca began, but Patrick interrupted her.

'Chris can have the treatment he requires with us. I'm going to gradually wean him off hard drugs. Initially, I'll put him on methadone tablets—that will reduce the withdrawal symptoms. We have a drug dependency consultant at our clinic in Brittany. The treatment I'm going to prescribe can be combined with the physiotherapy Chris needs for his leg.'

Patrick took out a large prescription pad and started

writing. Seconds later he looked up, glancing between Rebecca and Chris.

'I want to be quite sure this is what you want, Chris. You do want to be cured, don't you? If you do, it will mean being separated again from Rebecca. I don't want to move her from her obstetrics unit if I can help it. Of course, she'll be able to come down and visit you occasionally, and the sooner you get well again the sooner——'

'The sooner we can get married,' Chris interjected blandly. 'You just wait. I'll be a new man. Just give me a few weeks and you won't know me.'

Rebecca's heart dropped. How could she shatter Chris's illusions at this difficult time in his life? How could she tell him she had no intention of ever getting involved with him again? The young man she'd once thought she loved had long since vanished.

But most of all, regardless of how Patrick might have been involved in Florence's near death, she was still hopelessly in love with him.

CHAPTER ELEVEN

REBECCA and Patrick escorted Chris to La Colombière nursing home in Brittany the following weekend. Patrick had very carefully selected the correct combination of drugs to keep their patient from suffering too much from withdrawal symptoms, but at the same time weaning him off the dire need for hard drugs.

Chris's leg presented few problems. Rebecca was sure that with expert physiotherapy the muscles would be strengthened. The actual fracture of the mid-shaft of femur had healed beautifully, but it would take time before Chris would be able to walk without a limp.

Karine Griffon, the statuesque blonde physiotherapist, was waiting for them on their arrival at the nursing home. As soon as she saw Chris being helped out of the car she came forward to assist. When her new patient was standing in front of the house, the physiotherapist put her hands on his crutches.

'We'll get rid of these for a start,' she said casually. 'I've had a report from the radiologist concerning your X-rays, and there's no need to keep hobbling about like that. Stand up straight. . .put your good foot forward. . .heel, toe. . .now the other one. . .heel, toe. . .'

Rebecca's eyes met Patrick's and they both smiled. There seemed to be an instant rapport between Chris and his physiotherapist. Instead of Chris's usual stubborn resistance to advice, he was actually listening to Karine.

'Chris is positively hanging on Karine's every word,' Rebecca whispered to Patrick as they moved away from the impromptu physiotherapy session.

'If anyone can tame him, Karine Griffon will!' Patrick replied, as he pushed open the main door. 'Why do you think I wanted him to come down here?'

Rebecca smiled. 'I knew it was purely for medical reasons,' she told him.

He smiled back, the first as far as Rebecca could remember for days. It was so good to feel some of their tension easing off. They had hardly spoken to each other on the journey down, and when they had it was only some terse comment about their patient's welfare.

'What other reason could I have for wanting Chris here and you in Paris with me?' he asked in a neutral tone.

Her heart was beating rapidly as her dormant sensuality began to revive. She had gathered that Patrick had already discounted whatever it was that Chris had told him on the night of his untimely arrival from London. Patrick had obviously now deduced that Chris's ramblings about their strong relationship were purely figments of his imagination and probably drug-induced. But she would love to know what it was that Chris had said that had changed Patrick's attitude towards her.

She had tried so hard to ignore her feelings for Patrick during the last few days, but love was so difficult to deny. So Patrick's question now was purely rhetorical; no need to think up a reply when they both knew the answer.

They lunched with the rest of the staff at the long table overlooking the bay, with its spectacular view of the beach where Rebecca had played as a child. Memories came flooding back of that time long ago, long before she had met Chris and even longer before she had met Patrick.

'Penny for them,' whispered Patrick, while the staff conversation droned noisily around them. 'You're very quiet today.'

'I was remembering,' she replied softly. 'A time long ago when I was completely free. . .before the cares of the world came crowding in around me.'

'You'll be free again, Rebecca,' he murmured. 'We both will.'

For some unknown reason, she shivered. It was as if someone had walked over her grave. She wanted to be free. . .but not at the expense of somebody else. Urgently she looked up into Patrick's deep blue eyes, but they revealed nothing. The tenderness she saw was proof that he still loved her. . .as much as she loved him. . .but that solved nothing.

'What are you two whispering about?' Madame Thiret, the genial matron of La Colombière, enquired from the end of the table, with a benevolent smile.

Rebecca realised that the conversation had ceased and all eyes were upon them. Patrick, always capable of extricating himself from difficult situations, put on one of his charming smiles and told the staff that they were discussing the treatment of the new patient they had brought down. He asked them all to do their utmost to make the young man feel at home.

It was only then that Rebecca realised that Karine Griffon was missing from the table. As she realised that the physiotherapist must be taking her duties very seriously and working already with Chris, some of the weight began to slip from her shoulders.

She was even more relieved after a discussion with the drug dependency consultant, Monsieur Saumur. She listened in as he outlined his ideas on treatment with Patrick and Madame Thiret. Between them they came up with a workable programme. Monsieur Saumur agreed that he would come in from the local hospital a couple of times a week to check on Chris's progress and Madame Thiret would telephone him if there were any complications in the meantime.

Rebecca noticed that Madame Thiret had not mentioned the fact that she and Chris seemed to have broken off their engagement. If she thought their relationship was unusual she was professional enough not to comment about it, for which Rebecca was duly grateful.

Later that afternoon, as they took their leave, Rebecca found that Chris was not in the least despondent that she should be going back to Paris so soon.

He walked to the car, with Karine Griffon beside him, urging him to remember his posture and the correct movement of his feet.

'Don't worry about me, Rebecca,' he said non-chalantly. 'I think I'm going to like it here.' He turned to Karine. 'How soon before I can go swimming in the indoor pool?'

Karine glanced at Patrick, who gave a barely imperceptible nod. 'How about tomorrow?'

Chris let out a whoop of delight. 'Fantastic!'

For a brief moment Rebecca remembered the young man that Chris had been before falling in with the wrong crowd. It had been his enthusiasm for life that had first attracted her to him. But it had been his enthusiasm that had been his downfall. He was always easily led by others, and he liked to go along with whatever project his friends advocated, be it good or bad. He craved approval and hated to say no.

She knew it was just possible that his personality could return to what it had been. But life had moved on for her. Even if Chris were to be exactly as he had been all those years ago she couldn't love him again. . .not when her heart belonged to someone else.

She waved from the car. 'Take care of yourself, Chris.'

'Don't worry!' Karine called back. 'I'll look after him.'

She settled back against the comfortable leather seat and closed her eyes. They'd had an early start to the day and they would have a late arrival, possibly even early morning, back in Paris. She knew that Patrick would have preferred to stay on at La Colombière, but she was anxious to be back in the obstetrics unit as soon as possible. Henriette Dumas, one of her older ante-natal patients, was due to have her baby any day now, and she had promised to be there at the delivery if at all possible.

So if she shut her eyes before it was her turn to drive. . .

* * *

'Are you still with me?' Patrick's voice came to her as if from a dream. How long had she been asleep? She glanced at the clock on the dashboard. Heavens! They'd been on the road for a couple of hours. She rubbed her eyes.

'I'm sorry, I must have fallen asleep. Let me take a turn at the wheel.'

'No need, we're nearly there.' Patrick's voice was deliberately calm and soothing.

She glanced out of the window. Everything was dark; there were absolutely no lights on this road. It looked like a D-road, leading to the depths of the countryside. It certainly wasn't the main road back to Paris.

'We can't be nearly there, Patrick. Have you lost your way? Look, give me the map; I knew I should have kept awake.'

He laughed. 'Stop fussing! Everything's under control. We're booked in at the Lion d'Or in the next village. I made a couple of quiet phone calls while you were asleep—one to the Clinique to say we'd been held up and the other to this nice little country hotel I know. I'm far too tired to drive any further, and I don't feel like entrusting our lives to you this evening when you look as if you haven't slept for days.'

'But I need to get back to the Clinique in case Henriette Dumas goes into labour. You should have wakened me,' she began fretfully.

'Why? So that you could get your conscience ticking over and attempt to persuade me on a hazardous journey back to Paris? I spoke to Sister Taralon at the Clinique and she assured me that everything was quiet. Madame Dumas was sleeping peacefully. She could hold on for days, and her blood-pressure's come down. Still, if you want to get back you can take the train. I'll drop you off at the nearest railway station.'

Rebecca hated the sound of his impersonal tone. She knew she much preferred his casual, charming approach to the situation. As Patrick said, what was the point of getting her conscience to tick over? Brigitte Taralon would be in her element in charge of the obstetrics unit for the weekend. Henriette Dumas hadn't gone into labour. And another easing of her conscience was the fact that she had left Chris in good hands, as happy as she had seen him for a long time. So why not enjoy herself?

She glanced across at the stern profile at the wheel. 'I'm sorry, Patrick. It was sweet of you to book the hotel. I can't quite get used to the fact that I've got nothing to worry about and that here we are, just you and I, in the middle of nowhere, and. . .'

Patrick pulled the car to a halt on the grass verge with a wild screech of tyres. She had absolutely no time to wonder what was happening before his arms were around her and he was kissing her so passionately that all her cares and worries blew away into oblivion. Time ceased to exist. The world consisted of only two people, Patrick and herself.

The sound of a car approaching brought her back to earth and she pulled herself from the depths of her seat.

'Perhaps we should move on from here. . .' she began.

Patrick released her from his arms and started up the

engine again. 'I agree, we'd better move on. . .but let's remember where we'd got to. I'd just told you I loved you and you were about to tell me whether you loved me or not.'

Rebecca sighed. Her lips felt bruised from the passionate, almost savage onslaught of his kisses, but she knew she wanted more. . .much more. 'I'll tell you when you've explained what it was Chris said to you when he first arrived. He had you convinced that our engagement couldn't be broken at any price.'

The headlights of the car that had caught up with them shone into the car and she was able to make out Patrick's bemused expression.

'Cunning as a fox, your fiancé. . .or may I say ex-fiancé? He had me fooled by what he said. He told me that you'd been writing to him to say that one of the doctors was pestering you and that he'd better get himself to Paris as quickly as possible to put a stop to it. And he said I was not to be deceived by the fact that you'd seemed less than pleased to see him. He said you were madly in love with him, but you didn't know how to handle men who made a pass at you. He said it had happened before, but he'd always been there to save you and——'

Rebecca began to laugh. 'Chris has always had a vivid imagination, but he's surpassed himself this time. I suppose it was the drugs that had over-stimulated him, because, whatever else he does, he doesn't usually tell lies.'

Patrick took one hand from the wheel and took hold of hers as he deliberately slowed down the car on a wider stretch of road to enable the car behind them to pass. 'It was, quite definitely, the drugs. And I should have noticed the symptoms. I took everything he said as being true.'

'I should have noticed the change in Chris myself. But we were tired that night, if you remember. It had been a wonderful night out. . .the theatre, the restaurant. . .maybe it was the champagne that made us both so gullible.'

He squeezed her hand. 'It certainly was a wonderful night. . .and a sad way to end it. But we'll make up for it tonight.'

She longed to ask him what had happened after he had left her that night. Had he called in to see Florence as Edith claimed? And if so, what had happened to make Florence take an overdose? And, what was even worse. . .no, she dared not even think it. She had to trust Patrick, now that they'd found each other again. She couldn't break up this wonderful rapport between them. Better to ignore her unfounded suspicions.

They were approaching a small village. Dim lights twinkled behind drawn curtains at the cottage windows. They passed over a tiny hump-backed bridge and turned through a stone archway into the cobbled courtyard of the Lion d'Or.

An old man with a large electric torch came out of the kitchen, leaving the door wide open to reveal the welcome sight of food being prepared.

'*C'est vous, monsieur le docteur?*' the man called.

'*Oui c'est moi, Gaston.* Can you come and give me a hand with the luggage?'

'*Mais bien sûr!*' The old man hobbled across the

courtyard, his toothless mouth wide with a welcoming smile.

'My family have been calling in here for years,' Patrick explained to Rebecca as the old man bore down on them. 'Gaston is the odd-job man, and when I was a little boy he used to lift me up on to his shoulders and carry me down to the dairy to watch the cows being milked.'

'So we're not too far from the *autoroute* to Paris, then,' Rebecca commented, with a smile. 'I thought you'd carried me off into the middle of nowhere on purpose.'

He pretended to look shocked. 'Would I do such a thing to a fair young maid? What do you take me for, *mademoiselle*? This village used to be on the main road to Paris before the *autoroute* was built. . .ah, Gaston, *mon ami*. . .'

There was a noisy reunion between the doctor and the old man, and Rebecca was introduced as the doctor's assistant. As soon as Gaston was told that Rebecca was from England, he started to speak even louder and much more slowly.

She smiled and assured the old man that her French had improved a great deal in the last few months and she was able to understand him if he spoke in the normal way.

Patrick put his hand under Rebecca's arm and led her across the cobbles to the open kitchen door. Another reunion scene was enacted when *madame la cuisinière* left her cooking to embrace the doctor and chide him for not visiting the establishment for several years.

'But we're here now, Marianne,' Patrick said in a jovial tone. 'And we're hungry for some of your superb food. The finest restaurant in Paris can't compare with your cooking.'

After such a compliment, Marianne was overwhelmed, and hurried to find *monsieur le patron* to ensure that their distinguished client was given the very best in service.

Minutes later they were seated at a table in a quiet corner of the small hotel restaurant eating the most delicious *fruits de mer* that Rebecca had ever tasted. Marianne had assured them that the fish was fresh that day, and the delectable taste bore witness to the truth of this. The *fruits de mer* was followed by a succulent *faisan à la normande*—pheasant cooked in Calvados and cream, which was typical of the area of Normandy they were passing through. A *plateau de fromage* appeared, and then a mouthwatering dessert trolley, from which Rebecca chose *tarte aux abricots*.

They moved into the tiny salon set apart from the dining-room to drink their coffee. A new moon shone through the long casement window that led out to the garden. The grass was covered with a thin sprinkling of frost and the tall pine trees, illuminated in the moonlight, stood tall and ghostly in the sparkling frost.

Rebecca turned her attention from looking out into the garden to glance around the little salon. A heavily laden Christmas tree stood in one corner, and the old oak beams above them were festooned with festive streamers.

'Only a week to Christmas,' Rebecca said softly. 'I can feel myself caught up in the magic already. But I must admit, after the wonderful meal we've just had, there'd be magic in the air even without Christmas.'

Patrick leaned across from his chair, placing his coffee-cup on the table. They were quite alone, the other diners being still at the table or having left the restaurant.

'I think the magic comes from being together. I love you very much, Rebecca. You still haven't told me how you feel about me.'

Their eyes met and all her doubts and fears evaporated. 'I love you, Patrick,' she whispered softly.

His lips, when they claimed hers, were gentle and undemanding, unlike the desperately savage passion he'd shown earlier in the evening.

She closed her eyes, and gave in to the marvellous feeling that was stealing over her. The only way she could describe the feeling to herself was bliss. . .sheer bliss. . .it was as if she were floating on air.

A discreet cough from the entrance to the salon made her open her eyes and pull away from Patrick. Their kiss had been restrained, but still this wasn't the place for it! Patrick took hold of her arm and together they went out and climbed the ancient, uneven steps that led to the bedrooms.

Even the landing floor was sloping, first down and then up.

'I'm glad I haven't had too much to drink,' said Patrick. 'Otherwise I'd never be able to cope with this drunken floor.'

Rebecca giggled. They'd only had one glass of wine each because they wanted to make an early start back to Paris and knew they would need clear heads. But she felt intoxicated with the heady joy of her love for Patrick.

Their rooms were at the end of the landing, one either side, the doors facing each other. She had wondered about the sleeping arrangements, but had known that they would have to be perfectly proper in a place where Patrick was so well known. And she was glad. She didn't want to jump the gun; she didn't want there to be anything furtive about their relationship. It was enough to know that they loved each other and one day. . .one day they would be together. . . wouldn't they?

Patrick had both keys. He opened her door wide and stood on the threshold looking down at her.

'Goodnight, my love,' he whispered softly, as he bent to kiss her tenderly on the lips.

'Goodnight,' she murmured.

They stood for a moment, their arms locked around each other. Rebecca felt the terrible indecision of the moment as they looked into each other's eyes. She could only guess what was going through Patrick's mind. And suddenly she knew that she wanted to be in his arms for longer. . .oh, much longer than a goodnight kiss. She wanted to be sure of his love for her, to banish the awful doubts that lingered on at the back of her mind. If he asked her now. . .

But he had already drawn away from their embrace and stepped back towards the door of his room.

'*Dors bien*—sleep well, *chérie*,' he said softly.

And then he was gone. As she turned away and went into her room she felt a shiver of apprehension running through her. Patrick had told her he loved her; their

relationship seemed idyllic. . .but they weren't out of
the wood yet. There were too many obstacles in their
path. . .too many problems over which they had little
or no control.

CHAPTER TWELVE

THEY arrived back in Paris in time for lunch in the staff dining-room at the Clinique. As the conversation buzzed around Rebecca she glanced at Patrick, feeling suddenly the cold aloof attitude he always adopted when they were together in a professional capacity. It was as if he didn't want anyone to guess at their feelings for each other. As if he were keeping his options open.

'How was Brittany?' Blanche Souzan, the formidable night sister, always chose to have Sunday lunch at the Clinique when she had a weekend off. The young staff liked to joke that it was probably the social highlight of her week.

And indeed, the cuisine was as good as at many Paris restaurants. Today they were having *pintade aux champignons*—a succulent dish of guineafowl with mushrooms—but Rebecca thought it was sad that Blanche had nowhere else to go in her time off. Years of devotion to duty had left Mademoiselle Souzan in a lonely state, with no life of her own in her middle age.

'Brittany was as beautiful as ever,' Rebecca told her. 'My grandparents used to live down there, and I often visited them when I was a small child.'

'So I hear,' Sister Souzan said. 'Florence Maurin has told me all about you.'

Has she indeed? Rebecca thought, as she looked

across the table at her older colleague and wondered what else her arch-rival had disclosed.

Patrick stood up and excused himself from the table, murmuring something about patients to be seen. Rebecca followed suit, saying that she'd hurried back to be on hand for what might be a difficult delivery. But as she escaped through the dining-room door she could feel Blanche Souzan's eyes upon her.

Patrick was waiting for her in the corridor. 'You didn't hang around to hear what juicy gossip Florence has been spreading,' he said, with an amused smile.

'No fear! I can imagine what happens when those two get their heads together.'

'Would you consider a situation in which you could do more than imagine? I'd really like to invite the two of them to dinner along with our accountant, Jacques Fromentin, and Alain Laval. I need someone to play hostess. Florence would jump at the chance, but I don't want to ask her. . .for obvious reasons.'

Rebecca swung into step beside him as they walked along the corridor towards the lift. 'And just what are you cooking up, Patrick?' she asked shrewdly.

'Oh, I haven't given the menu a thought yet. I can get the caterers in, and the daily help, my *femme de ménage*——'

'I'm not talking about the food,' she interposed. 'I can't imagine why you'd want to get all these people together. You must have an ulterior motive other than social duty.'

He laughed. 'I didn't know I was so transparent. You're right, I do have an ulterior motive, but I can't tell you what it is—yet.'

'Well, thanks for your vote of confidence. I'm not sure whether I want to play hostess for you.'

He paused by the lift. There was no one about and he bent down and brushed her cheek with his lips. 'Please don't ask any questions. . .and please be my hostess.'

She gave a wry grin. 'Provided you tell me what you're up to, Patrick Delan.'

He put a long tapering finger under her chin. The smile on his lips melted her heart and, in spite of herself, she felt herself falling for his charms again.

'One day, my love,' he whispered.

They parted outside Obstetrics. Intrigued by the prospect of the strange dinner party, Rebecca agreed to be Patrick's hostess. She realised that one of her reasons for wanting to attend was that she'd never actually seen Patrick's apartment. In three whole months she'd never had the doubtful pleasure of looking around the rooms where he had lived with his wife. But her curiosity was mixed with apprehension. It wasn't anything she could put her finger on. . .just an awful nagging feeling that something would go wrong.

Brigitte Taralon had run the obstetrics department admirably. Rebecca was pleased to find that nothing had suffered in her absence. So much for believing herself to be indispensable!

But during the afternoon, as she caught up with the written report in her office, the red light flashed, indicating that Henriette Dumas wanted someone in her room immediately.

Rebecca was on her feet and hurrying along the corridor in seconds. Her thirty-nine-year-old first-time mother was sitting on the edge of the bed holding her abdomen.

'My waters have broken,' she announced in a strained voice.

Rebecca took charge of the situation, assuring her patient that all would be well if she relaxed on her bed and took it easy. She examined her abdomen for signs of contractions, took her blood-pressure and checked the foetal heartbeat before again reassuring her that there was no need to worry.

Back in her office she called Patrick and asked him to come up to Obstetrics. 'It's Henriette Dumas. The membranes have ruptured, but there's no sign of a contraction and her blood-pressure is rising. The foetus doesn't seem distressed as yet, but. . .'

'I'm just on my way into surgery,' Patrick told her. 'An emergency ectopic. I'll be with you in an hour at the latest. If you're unduly worried call Alain. It sounds as if we may have to induce.'

Rebecca continued to monitor her patient closely, trying not to appear worried. The blood-pressure had begun to rise sharply. She checked the foetus; the foetal heartbeat was still normal. She breathed a sigh of relief and went away to attend to a new mother who was having a problem with breast-feeding. As she soothed and coaxed this patient her mind was on the patient who had yet to be delivered.

She glanced at the clock. It was nearly an hour since she'd rung Patrick. She dared not wait any longer. Excusing herself, she went back to Madame Dumas's room and checked on the foetus. She could now detect signs of foetal distress, but there were still no contractions. As she raised herself from the examination she heard the door open and Patrick walked in, still in his surgical gown with his mask hanging loosely around his neck.

'I came as quickly as I could,' he began breathlessly.

'We'd better induce,' Rebecca said quietly, turning away from the patient.

Within seconds, after a quick examination, Patrick nodded in agreement. Rebecca had already prepared the equipment in anticipation of an induction being necessary. Now she began to set up the IV, while Patrick found a suitable vein in the patient's hand in which to insert the cannula.

'You're going to feel some discomfort,' he told Henriette Dumas. 'Would you like me to give you an epidural anaesthetic so that you don't feel anything?'

Madame Dumas hesitated. 'How long will the induction take?'

'Two, maybe three hours. The contractions are pretty intense towards the end of the delivery, so. . .'

'Oh, I can stand two or three hours,' the patient said cheerily. 'I'd really like to know what's going on. I've practised my ante-natal exercises, you know.'

'Well, if you change your mind,' said Patrick, 'I'll be on hand to help you.'

Rebecca's eyes met his. She knew they were both thinking the same thing. It so often happened that a new, inexperienced mother thought she understood the intensity of the final contractions, but when it came to the crunch got into a panic and pleaded for anaesthesia.

'I'll keep my eye on her,' Rebecca told Patrick when they were back in the office. 'One of the nurses will stay with her the whole time and I'll be there at a moment's notice if she needs me. Are you free for the delivery?'

Patrick nodded. 'I'll settle my post-operative ectopic and then I'll be with you until after the birth.'

'I hope there are no complications,' Rebecca said. 'Henriette's been trying for a baby for years. She'd almost given up hope and planned to adopt.'

'Stop worrying,' he told her. 'She's going to get the best care and attention. If it's humanly possible we'll deliver a healthy baby. What does she want—a girl or a boy?'

Rebecca gave a weak smile. 'She doesn't mind, so long as it's fit and healthy.'

It's a boy!' As Patrick pronounced the exciting news, two hours later, a sigh of relief ran round the delivery-room. It had been a quick delivery, but the induced contractions had been exceptionally strong.

Rebecca sponged the sweat from her patient's face, dabbing it dry with a soft fluffy towel. 'You were great, Henriette,' she said soothingly. 'I couldn't have performed better myself.'

Henriette Dumas gave a happy smile. 'You wait till it's your turn, Sister. You won't believe just what hard work it is. I feel exhausted.'

'Perhaps I'll stick to delivering babies and leave the production to others,' smiled Rebecca, as she picked up the warm, damp little bundle, still wrapped in a dressing sheet, and handed the baby to its proud mother.

Tears of joy streamed down Henriette's face as she

looked down at her new son. 'There's nothing to
compare with a moment like this,' she whispered. 'I've
never been so happy. Will somebody go and fetch my
husband, please?'

'He's on his way,' Patrick assured her.

Rebecca looked at him and they both smiled.
Henriette's husband had left the delivery-room half an
hour before the birth, unable to bear the sight of his
wife's struggles. From the case-notes, Rebecca had
gathered that Monsieur Dumas, now in his mid-forties,
had been ill prepared for fatherhood. Although they
had been married for years, his lifestyle had changed
very little from when he'd been a well-heeled bachelor,
able to please himself all the time. And, while his wife
was desperately hoping for a baby, his own thoughts
on the matter were probably in the other direction!

Gilbert Dumas now came hesitantly into the room
and gazed, wide-eyed, almost in disbelief at the sight
of his wife holding their son. Patrick put his arm around
the smaller man's back and led him towards the delivery bed.

Initially, he appeared dumbstruck. But after a few
minutes of assessing the situation he raised his head
and looked around the room. 'I'd like to thank you all
for your participation in this, the happiest event of our
lives,' he said.

Rebecca warmed to the new father. His small speech
sounded as if he were addressing the board of directors
of which he was chairman, but his heart was in the
right place. He would soon get used to the disruption
of their well-ordered lives, and Henriette Dumas would
get the support she needed and deserved. There was

something magical about having a baby. The baby arrived, wanted or unwanted, and immediately changed the lives of everyone around it. It came equipped with a fantastic set of lungs enabling it to make its needs obvious and, what was more important, it brought its love with it. There were few people in the world who could ignore the precious feeling of love that a baby induced.

As these maternal ideas flooded through her mind Rebecca realised that she was getting broody! She glanced across at Patrick as he pulled on a fresh mask and prepared to work on the patient's placenta. When her time came to have babies she hoped against hope that the father would be someone as wonderful as Patrick.

She hardly dared to wish that it would be Patrick. It seemed like wishing for the moon. But she told herself that miracles did happen. She wasn't going to give up easily.

Patrick had scheduled his dinner party for Christmas Eve. As he explained to Rebecca, this was probably a good time to have it from a staffing point of view. Only emergency patients would be admitted and most of their patients would have gone home for Christmas. The Clinique would be relatively quiet.

A cook had been hired for the evening, and Rebecca was beginning to wonder what it was she was actually expected to do. When she arrived early in the evening, she found Patrick's daily *femme de ménage*, Madame Julian, setting the elegant table and *madame la cuisinière* installed in the kitchen.

Patrick led her across the large expanse of his thickly carpeted sitting-room towards a balcony that looked out over the illuminated garden. From high up there in the penthouse suite it was possible to catch a glimpse of the lights shining on to the Seine and the Rive Gauche beyond. All around, the attic windows and eaves of the tall buildings mingled together, giving the impression of a superior world, reaching up into the sky, remote and set apart from the mundane, everyday life that existed in the streets down below.

Rebecca took hold of the iron railing that ran around the balcony and smiled. 'It's so beautiful up here, Patrick.'

He came up behind her and put his hands on her shoulders. 'Don't catch cold out here. Your dress is rather flimsy.'

She turned. 'Do you like it?' She'd spent a couple of hours in Galeries Lafayette trying on dress after dress until she'd found the one she felt was exactly right for the occasion. It was a high price to pay for such a small, frivolous piece of chiffon, but she'd fallen in love with it as soon as she saw it.

'Of course I like it,' he told her, with a smile. 'Red suits you. . .you should wear it more often. And you have such pretty shoulders that need to be shown off.' His fingers ran lightly across the bare skin on either side of the slender straps. 'And you're taller.'

Rebecca laughed as he glanced down at the red satin high heels. 'I hope you won't expect me to run around in these. I can walk in them if. . .'

'You look like an elegant Parisian model tonight,' he told her, his eyes shining with admiration.

She was glad she had taken such trouble over her appearance. It had been worth it. 'What exactly do my duties as hostess involve?' she asked quickly.

Patrick smiled. 'Nothing domestic, I assure you. The cook and my *femme de ménage* will see to the food. I want you to make sure that everyone relaxes and enjoys themselves. Let me know if you feel there's any friction between guests and that sort of thing. And above all, just be your charming self. Everyone will love you!'

Rebecca remembered Blanche Souzan and Florence. 'Well, perhaps not everyone!' she said, with a wry grin.

'I want you to be particularly attentive to Jacques Fromentin, our accountant,' Patrick told her. 'He's looking forward to meeting you.'

'Oh, yes, I remember Madame Thiret talking about him the first time we were down in Brittany. I gather he can be difficult in allocating the Clinique funds. Is this what the dinner's all about?' she asked, with a mischievous smile.

'Of course not,' he replied dismissively. 'We got that sorted out weeks ago. After all, at the end of the day, I hold the purse-strings. No, what I have in mind has nothing to do with finance.'

'Patrick, you're being much too mysterious. Why won't you tell me what you're up to?'

The sound of voices at the door made him hold up his hand. 'Not now, please, Rebecca. Be patient and trust me.'

She clenched her hands in frustration. Why did he have to reiterate the words 'trust me'? It was so infuriating.

She took a deep breath, put on her charming hostess smile and followed Patrick to the door.

It was Jacques Fromentin. A tall, distinguished-looking man in his late forties, he came into the sitting-room with a broad smile on his unseasonally suntanned face. Rebecca thought immediately that he looked like the sort of man who enjoyed the good things of life, champagne, women, fast cars, skiing down dangerous slopes, probably piloting his own aircraft. She noticed the brown stains at the end of his fingers as he extended his hand and smelt expensive cigars as he leaned forward to kiss her hand in a very masculine, Gallic gesture.

'*Mademoiselle, je suis enchanté de faire votre connaissance.*' The words tripped lightly off his tongue.

A real charmer! Rebecca thought as she smiled back. But not her type! The woman who became ensnared with a man like this would have to keep her wits about her.

Patrick handed them each a glass of champagne and suggested Rebecca take care of Jacques while he saw to the ladies who were just arriving. Rebecca glanced nervously over towards the door as Blanche Souzan and Florence came into the room.

'Tell me,' Jacques Fromentin was saying to her, 'are you enjoying your work here at the Clinique?'

Rebecca's eyes were still on the little group by the door as she answered, 'Yes, I find it utterly absorbing, and such good experience from a medical point of view.'

'And you plan to stay on in Paris for some time?' Monsieur Fromentin pursued.

Rebecca took a sip of her champagne. 'Ah, that will depend, Monsieur Fromentin.'

'Please call me Jacques, and I will call you Rebecca, if I may. As I was saying, on what will it depend?'

She took a deep breath. 'On circumstances. . .ah, Florence, how nice to see you again! Do you know Monsieur Jacques Fromentin?'

Rebecca was ill prepared for the look of displeasure on Florence's face. She noticed that Madame Maurin had lost weight since the unfortunate incident that had ended up with the gastric lavage. This gave her a wizened look that was utterly different from the chic appearance she had had when Rebecca had first seen her out on her balcony three months ago. And the expression that spread over her pallid face as she stared at Jacques Fromentin was anything but becoming.

It was at this point that Rebecca noticed Florence's private nurse moving quickly across the room. Dressed in an elegant cocktail gown, Diane Poitiers looked as if she was just another guest at the dinner party, but Rebecca decided she must be there in attendance on Florence, who looked far from well.

If Jacques Fromentin found anything strange in Florence's demeanour he ignored it and rose to the occasion, announcing that yes, he and Florence had already met.

'It's a long time since I had the pleasure of seeing you, Madame Maurin,' he continued, holding out his hand towards her.

Florence ignored the gesture but told him she had been ill and out of circulation for a while.

'I'm sorry to hear it. Nothing serious, I hope?'

Patrick joined the group and poured more champagne into Jacques Fromentin's glass. 'Florence had a very bad bout of gastro-enteritis. Nurse Diane Poitiers has been nursing her back to health.'

Nurse Poitiers gave a reserved smile but offered no more to the conversation, which switched to preparations for Christmas Day and arrangements for festivities in the Clinique.

As Rebecca moved between the guests, ensuring that no one was neglected, she could feel an undercurrent of disharmony. The jovial Alain Laval arrived and helped to break the ice somewhat, but Rebecca didn't know how she could inject a little more warmth into the atmosphere. Blanche Souzan remained cold and aloof at the edge of the group, nervously twisting her champagne glass as she tried to sip the effervescent liquid. She had already insisted that she didn't like champagne, but she would give it a try, just this once.

Rebecca moved out on to the balcony for a breath of fresh air. The depressing atmosphere was making her feel claustrophobic. Seconds later, the delicate hint of Patrick's cologne made her turn her head from the twinkling landscape.

'Playing truant?' he asked, with a wry grin.

She smiled. 'I'm sorry, I just had to get away for a few moments. I'll come back in now.'

But he caught her arm as she started to move inside. 'Stay for a moment—we both need a breather.'

She looked up into his deep blue eyes and whispered, 'Why, Patrick? Why have you called this odd assortment together? You didn't need a hostess, you needed the Corps Diplomatique!'

He stifled a laugh. 'You're doing great. Don't give up now—I promise, it will be worth it.'

She groaned. 'I'd better go and see what's happening in the kitchen.'

'It's all under control. Madame Julian is already changed into her maid's uniform. She'll serve the delicacies that Cook has produced and I'll keep pouring the wine. You just keep the conversation flowing.'

For an instant he held her against him. Through the flimsy chiffon of her dress she could feel his heart beating rapidly. He was nervous. . .yes, he was as nervous and apprehensive as she was. So what was he up to. . .and why was he keeping it secret?

CHAPTER THIRTEEN

REBECCA felt nothing but relief when an emergency call from the Clinique broke up the ill-fated dinner party. A call from the junior night sister expressing concern about Dr Delan's post-operative ectopic patient sent Blanche Souzan scurrying towards the door, demanding her coat and stating loudly that she couldn't trust her young assistant.

Patrick reluctantly helped Sister Souzan into her ancient fur coat, saying, however, that there was absolutely no reason why she shouldn't stay on at the dinner party. He was going to go back to the Clinique, but he didn't want the other guests to depart. Rebecca would continue to act as hostess until his return.

'I know where my duty lies, Dr Delan,' declared Blanche Souzan importantly. 'But I agree with you that Sister Manson should remain here.'

Rebecca caught Patrick's pleading look as he escorted the obdurate night sister away from the party. His lips were mouthing the words, 'Please stay!'

And so Rebecca stayed on for a further hour until one by one the guests departed. First, Alain Laval had excused himself, pleading an early duty at the Clinique on Christmas morning. Then Diane Poitiers said she would go down to the apartment to prepare Madame Maurin's bed and medication. She had suggested that *madame* might like to accompany her, but Florence

149

gave her a withering look that indicated she should hold her tongue.

And so, eventually, after Rebecca had dismissed the *femme de ménage* and the *cuisinière*, thanking the latter for the delicious *canard à l'orange* and all the other gastronomic delights, she found herself alone with Jacques Fromentin and Florence.

The three of them were in the centre of the large sitting-room, staring at each other as they attempted to resurrect the already exhausted conversation.

Why doesn't Florence go home? Rebecca thought despairingly as she went out to the kitchen to make some more coffee. What's she waiting for?

As she poured out final cups of coffee, Rebecca wondered if Florence was still hoping to ensnare Patrick. That would explain the hostile glances directed in her direction.

'Would you like me to escort you back to your apartment, Madame Maurin?' Jacques Fromentin asked after a particularly lengthy pause in the conversation.

Rebecca watched Florence's reaction. First she looked taken aback, almost affronted at the offer, and then she gave a wan smile of acceptance.

'Perhaps it would be a good idea if I retired. I must admit, I'm beginning to feel sleepy,' she said, in the soft voice she used to indicate how weak she was feeling.

Rebecca sprang to her feet. 'I'll fetch your wrap.'

There were polite murmurs indicating that it had been a delightful evening as Rebecca performed her

final hostess duty. As she closed the door on the last
two guests she breathed an audible sigh of relief.

Seconds later the phone rang. It was Patrick. 'Don't
go,' he requested when she said she was finally alone.
'I've finished off here. My patient's out of danger
again. I'll have to come back early in the morning, but
I need to unwind. Please stay on, Rebecca. Pour
yourself a drink and put your feet up. You deserve to
take it easy. I don't know what I would have done
without you.'

'You didn't need me, Patrick,' she said sagely.
'There was nothing anyone could have done to thaw
the ice with such an ill-assorted gathering, but the food
was superb.' She hesitated. 'Won't you tell me what
you're up to?'

'If you wait right there,' he replied softly.

Her heart began to beat rapidly as she put down the
receiver and went back across the thick carpet. She
closed the long casement window that led out on to the
balcony. It had been opened for a few minutes to air
the room after the cloying smell of Jacques Fromentin's
cigars, but the cold night air was too much for her now.
She snuggled down into the depths of the large sofa
that dominated the centre of the room, kicking off her
high-heeled shoes.

She felt she had expended more nervous energy that
evening than she normally used in a whole week on
duty! There was a champagne bucket on the table
beside her. She reached out her hand and poured some
into a glass.

She took a sip as she leaned back amid the cushions
feeling decidedly decadent, awaiting a man in his apart-

ment after midnight and drinking his champagne! She
put down her glass on the table, deciding that she would
close her eyes for a few minutes until Patrick arrived. . .

'Patrick, I'm not asleep. I was waiting for you.'
Rebecca sat up, disorientated, rubbing her eyes with
one hand as she smoothed the wrinkles out of her new
chiffon dress with the other.

He sat down on the sofa beside her and reached
down to push a lock of hair from her eyes. 'You look
exhausted. I shouldn't have insisted you stay on. It's
an hour since I rang you. I had to go back to my patient
and then when I phoned again there was no reply. Let
me take you back to your room.'

'No! You promised to explain.' She was instantly
wide awake, shaking off the last vestige of her weariness. 'I've spent a whole evening torturing myself; you
needn't think you can duck out of it now.'

He gave her a wry grin. 'I'll go and make some
coffee and——'

'No, Patrick, be still and put me out of my misery!'

He hesitated. 'Well, first you'd better tell me what
happened to Florence at the end of the evening. Did
she go home alone?'

Rebecca gave a puzzled frown. 'As a matter of fact,
Jacques Fromentin offered to escort her as Nurse
Poitiers had already left.'

Patrick smiled. 'Good! Splendid! That's what I
hoped would happen.'

'But, Patrick. . .' Rebecca paused in mid-sentence
as the light began to dawn. 'You're matchmaking,
aren't you? You're trying to get those two together?

Trying to. . .' She stopped short, realising that she'd been about to imply that Patrick wanted to get Florence off his hands. But that would be too direct, and too distressing, especially if Patrick had been in any way involved in Florence's recent drug overdose.

As she thought about that near-fatal event, she felt a shiver of anxiety. How far would Patrick go to achieve his own ends? Did he possess a ruthless streak that she didn't know about? Looking at him now, his suave consultant image, the caring, expert doctor whom all the patients adored, who would think there might be a sinister side to his character?

Certainly not she! She had to believe in him, in the man she had come to love so much.

She reached out and touched the side of his face, tracing one of the laughter lines around his mouth. 'I don't think there's much hope of those two getting together,' she told him softly. 'They don't even like each other. Florence looked as if he was the last person she'd hoped to see when she first arrived, and they were barely civil to each other until——'

'Until it came to going home,' Patrick interrupted, with a ring of triumph in his voice. 'You can't always tell what people think about each other just by watching them. Take you and me, for instance. Which one of the staff at the Clinique would suspect that we were in love with each other?'

'No one in their right mind, I agree,' she agreed, evenly. 'You're always at such pains to be professional at the Clinique. And even here, in your own apartment, when the Clinique staff are here you're deliberately cool with me. You were at great pains to explain to everyone that my appointment as hostess tonight was just an extension of my nursing duties. I felt like the hired hand.'

'Oh, my darling!' He pulled her into his arms and covered her face with kisses. 'I'm so sorry. I thought that was how you would want me to explain why you were here.'

Between kisses she came up for air and looked up into the tender eyes that were watching her with a solicitous expression. She hadn't meant to complain about his behaviour towards her, but in the heat of the moment it had all come out.

She put her finger on his mouth to prevent any more kisses. Delicious as it was, she wanted to get to the truth of the situation.

'So do you admit to playing Cupid this evening?' she asked him.

The smile on his face was decidedly boyish. She hardened her heart and pursed her lips. 'As I said, you're wasting your time,' she continued. 'They're not remotely interested in each other. I gathered that their paths have crossed before, but do they really know each other?' she asked.

An enigmatic smile crossed his lips. 'Oh, yes, they most certainly do. The situation is not at all as it seemed tonight.' He took a deep breath. 'I think they can be persuaded back to a relationship.'

'Back to a relationship?' Rebecca queried. 'What sort of a relationship did they have?'

He hesitated before answering. 'The usual. But there were complications. . .' He broke off, frowning. 'I can't discuss it. All I can tell you is that there's a possibility of a reconciliation if we help fate along. Now, would you be willing to go out with Jacques, if I could arrange it? Florence could be coaxed into becoming interested in him if she was jealous of you. I've never known a woman who always coveted what someone else had as much as Florence does.'

She ran a hand through her long auburn hair in a gesture of exasperation. 'Patrick, this is all too devious. I can't think why you should imagine that Florence being jealous of me might get them together. And the answer to your question is no, I won't go out with Jacques. Besides which, it's none of your business. Jacques Fromentin is a mature, sophisticated man. He obviously will choose who he wants to go out with.'

'Ah, but he can be pointed in the right direction,' Patrick rejoined smoothly. 'And I saw the way he looked at you this evening. Admiration was dancing in his eyes at one point. I went out of the room for a moment and when I returned I saw the way he was looking at you across the table. I was terribly jealous.'

She swallowed as she felt her pulses racing. 'You were jealous because of me, Patrick?' she said slowly.

He gave her a puzzled frown. 'Of course I was. You know how I feel about you.'

She snuggled against him. 'No, I don't. I'm completely at sea about the situation. You'd better enlighten me.'

He pulled her against him, stroking her hair, as his lips reached down to claim hers. 'Words are so inadequate,' he whispered as he locked her into his passionate embrace. . .

* * *

She was awakened by the sound of the bells from the church of Ste-Catherine floating in through the partially opened window. She glanced around at the crumpled sheets as she began to remember. Oh, it had been such a heavenly end to the awful evening! And it had seemed the most natural thing in the world that Patrick should sweep her into his arms and carry her off to his bedroom.

She pulled herself up amid the soft pillows and stretched languorously as she allowed her mind to linger on the early morning hours. At last she felt she was sure of Patrick's love for her. . .and she would do anything now to keep it.

She looked around at the elegant bedroom with its sumptuous drapes, which complemented the Louis Quinze furniture to perfection, and for a few moments she felt insecure. Was this the room he had shared with his wife? There were no photographs, no mementoes. It was as impersonal as a luxury hotel suite. Had he loved his wife. . .as much as he had professed, in the early hours of this morning, to loving herself?

The door opened and Patrick walked in carrying a silver tray. Rebecca could smell the aroma of hot coffee and fresh-baked croissants as he padded across the carpet to set the tray down on her bedside table. His hair was still rumpled, his feet were bare and the white towelling robe reached only to mid-thigh, revealing his long, muscular, athletic legs, the skin coloured with the remnants of last year's suntan. She thought he seemed like a little boy having a day off from school as he turned to look at her. It was as if he thought she might have disappeared overnight.

'I persuaded the concierge to go along to the *boulangerie* for me,' he said, in a matter-of-fact voice. Then suddenly his expression softened as he leaned towards her and kissed her gently on the lips. 'I'm glad you stayed, Rebecca. Happy Christmas!'

'Happy Christmas!' she replied, savouring the sensual excitement his lips induced. This morning he only had to come near her to set her pulses racing as she remembered the bliss of their lovemaking.

He poured coffee from the silver percolator and handed her a cup. She drank deeply, suddenly realising that she was very thirsty and starving hungry. It had been a long time since dinner last night. . .it had been a lifetime. And so much had changed. She felt like a different person. She certainly wasn't the ingénue who'd arrived to play hostess.

'You're very quiet,' he commented.

Rebecca smiled up at him as she reached for another croissant. 'I'm terribly hungry,' she told him. 'I was just thinking it had been a long time since dinner. . .and I ate very little,' she added, her cheeks suddenly suffused with a blush.

He laughed as he pulled her against his side. 'No regrets, I hope?'

She shook her head and took another sip of coffee. 'My only regret is that I put myself down for duty today. I feel like taking a day off, lingering on over my breakfast for once.'

'So do I,' he said softly. 'But at least we'll be together.'

'But everything will change once we're inside the

Clinique,' Rebecca said realistically. 'The magic dream
will be shattered.'

Patrick cupped her face with his hand. 'Did it seem
like a magic dream, Rebecca?'

She nodded. 'I'm so afraid the dream will end and
we'll wake up and have to come down to earth again.'

'We have to help the dream to continue into reality,'
he told her fervently. 'We've got to free ourselves of
commitments. Look, if you won't agree to seeing
Jacques by yourself, let me set up a foursome. We'll
have a night out with Florence and Jacques. All I ask
is that you flirt with Jacques so that he pays you a few
compliments—as he will. He's a real lady's man. When
you see Florence taking notice you can back off and
we'll be home and dry.'

'Patrick, there must be an easier way of disposing of
Florence. . .oh, sorry!' She checked herself as she saw
the pained expression on his face. 'I know you promised her husband to take care of her, before he died,
but surely she can stand on her own two feet by now?'

A look of infinite sadness crossed his face. 'That's
where you're wrong, Rebecca.' He hesitated. 'You
may have thought it strange when I hired a private
nurse to take care of Florence after. . .after that unfortunate incident. What you didn't realise was that Nurse
Poitiers is no ordinary nurse. She's a highly skilled
psychiatric nurse, working in conjunction with one of
the top psychiatrists in France. And the reports she's
given me so far have borne out the wisdom of what
Michel, her husband, told me shortly before he died.'

Rebecca had put down her cup and was hanging on
Patrick's words. The revelation that Nurse Poitiers was

a psychiatric nurse had come as a complete shock. But now everything was beginning to fall into place. The jigsaw was taking shape.

'What did Michel tell you?' she asked apprehensively.

He took a deep breath and his eyes, on her face, were sad and troubled. 'Michel told me that Florence's father had committed suicide when she was a tiny child. . .before she could even remember him. She was raised by her mother, a hard, domineering woman who refused to have men in the house after the death of Florence's father. Florence was therefore virtually starved of male company until she ran away in her teens to join a theatre group and become an actress. When she discovered she enjoyed male company, she found she couldn't get enough of them. She went from man to man, revelling in her new-found sensuality but searching. . .all the time searching and not knowing what it was she needed. Then Michel came along, and she fell in love. He told me he realised from the start that Florence couldn't live without a man. . .but she had to fall in love with him. And once she loved a man, he mustn't let her down.'

Rebecca was silent for a few seconds as she realised the implications of his words. 'You're carrying an impossible burden, Patrick,' she told him.

'It's not impossible!' She blanched at the sound of his vehement voice and saw the determination in his eyes. 'I have to find a good man for Florence, or. . .'

'Or what?' she asked.

He turned away from her and she could no longer read the expression in his eyes. He remained silent,

just as she had known he would, and the troubled
suspicions returned to torment her.

'But what makes you think that Jacques will be a
good match for Florence?' she asked. 'He looks something of a playboy to me.'

He gave a wry grin. 'That's the impression he likes
to create at the moment. But he was faithful to his first
wife until her death some years ago. And I have reason
to believe that if Florence and Jacques could solve their
differences they would be very happy together. I think
we should certainly try to help them along their way,
otherwise. . .'

She shivered as he stopped again, mid-sentence.
There was no alternative but to go along with his plan.

'All right, you win. Set up the foursome,' she told
him.

He bent down and kissed her lightly on the cheek.
'You won't regret it,' he whispered. 'Remember you're
doing it for us. Our whole future is at stake.'

CHAPTER FOURTEEN

CHRISTMAS DAY at the Clinique started out quiet and uneventful. Most of the patients who were able had opted for going home, even if it meant returning after the festivities. There were a couple of premature babies in incubators requiring Rebecca's constant attention, otherwise she was able to relax and enjoy the festive spirit. She had given all her nurses the day off except one trained nurse who had recently separated from her husband and had requested to work all day, not wanting to find herself alone on a day when everyone was supposed to be with their loved ones.

Patrick called in around lunchtime to invite Rebecca down to the dining-room for roast turkey. She agreed to leave the obstetrics unit for an hour on condition that her nurse called her if she was worried about the prems.

The dining-room was festooned with coloured streamers and balloons. Sister Souzan waved to them as they entered, indicating that she had saved seats on her table.

'A superb dinner party, Dr Delan,' Blanche Souzan announced as Patrick sat down dutifully beside her. Rebecca was forced to sit on the other side of the night sister, so that if she wanted to speak to Patrick she would have to peer around the ample bosom.

The other medical staff looked suitably impressed that Sister Souzan had got herself an invitation to Dr Delan's apartment. It was widely known that he was choosy about whom he invited on the rare occasions he had entertained since his wife died. It had been rumoured that he was going to marry the widow of Dr Maurin, who had been killed in the car driven by his wife, but the situation seemed to have reached an impasse. Nevertheless, the Clinique grapevine was always ready to pick up on any snippet of information regarding their handsome and illustrious medical director.

And it just so happened that the young sister sitting on Rebecca's other side had heard rumours concerning Madame Maurin's health and now jumped at the chance of pumping Rebecca.

'Were you at the dinner party last night, Sister Manson?' she asked in a bland tone.

Rebecca turned to look at her colleague. Béatrice Dupond was one of those people who usually remained silent at the table, and Rebecca doubted if she'd exchanged more than half a dozen words with her since arriving at the Clinique.

'Yes, I was there,' she said, helping herself from the serving dish of *pommes frites* that was being circulated.

'And I suppose Madame Maurin was there?'

Rebecca carefully replaced the serving spoon on to the dish. 'Yes, she was, as a matter of fact. . .is she a friend of yours, Sister Dupond?'

The young woman smiled. 'No. My connection with her is purely professional. When I was a girl, I attended the same *lycée* as Diane Poitiers, her private nurse, and when we meet Diane likes to discuss her work with me.' She lowered her voice. 'I think it's scandalous the way they're trying to cover things up.'

Rebecca could feel an increase in her breathing, but she tried to remain calm, although intensely aware that Blanche Souzan had turned to listen in to the conversation. Béatrice Dupond had spoken in rapid French, but Rebecca had understood every word only too well. Still, there was no harm in playing the idiot foreigner if it meant she didn't have to give an opinion on the subject of Florence's mystery illness.

She frowned. '*Comment? Je ne comprends pas.* I don't understand.' Then, picking up the serving dish, she turned her back on the inquisitive colleague and offered to serve Sister Souzan. Her fingers trembled as she spooned *pommes frites* on to the night sister's plate. Raising her eyes, she saw that Patrick was watching her, a troubled expression in his dark blue eyes.

She turned away, knowing it had only been a matter of time before the rumours gathered momentum. But she was determined not to add to them. Her lips were sealed. She knew where her loyalty lay. She only hoped it wasn't misplaced.

But later, when she came off duty, she found Patrick waiting to take her back to her cosy little *chambre de bonne*. She invited him in and made coffee on her small electric stove. When she had first taken the room, at Florence's instigation, she had thought it was a poky little place. But now, with the addition of a couple of plants in terracotta pots and a crystal vase filled with fresh flowers, new curtains bought in the sale at Printemps, it was beginning to feel like home.

As she turned to give Patrick a cup of coffee, she saw he was holding out a small parcel towards her. She had wondered when—or indeed if—they were going to exchange Christmas presents. Now, as she opened the small, expensive jewel case bearing the name of an exclusive jewellers in the Faubourg St-Honoré, she felt a sudden rush of pure happiness. The gold chain which lay in a bed of silk was simplicity and perfection at one and the same time. What exquisite taste Patrick had!

She expressed her thanks as he leaned down and clasped the chain around her neck.

'I'll always wear it,' she whispered, watching his expression in the mirror.

His enigmatic eyes gave nothing away, but she sensed the pleasure her reaction had given him. By comparison, she felt her own gift to Patrick, of a silk scarf—far the most expensive scarf she'd ever bought!—paled into insignificance. But he smiled and knotted it around his neck, and she thought he looked even more handsome.

He left her soon afterwards, saying he had to return to the Clinique to check on the emergency ectopic patient. As they kissed goodbye at the door to her room, Rebecca felt the sadness of parting, even though it was going to be for only a few hours. She realised that she was becoming more and more dependent on this man, and, the more her love increased, the more apprehensive she felt. She felt it was too good to last.

She leaned against the closed door, listening to the sound of his footsteps disappearing. Unconsciously, one hand reached up to finger the gold chain. Surely this was tangible proof that Patrick loved her. . .or was it simply a gift to ensure her loyalty to him?

*   *   *

Almost a week went by before Patrick was able to arrange the foursome that Rebecca was dreading. They had both been busy during the days that followed Christmas. There had been a general influx of new patients and a returning of those who had gone home to be with their families but now had to resume medical treatment.

When she met Patrick in the corridor on New Year's Eve he gave her a triumphant smile.

'It's all set for tonight. I know you're free, because I checked the off-duty list.'

'What's all set for tonight?' she asked, with a wide-eyed innocent stare.

'Come on, Rebecca! I know you haven't forgotten your promise to go out with Florence and Jacques. It took a great deal of persuasion on my part,' he replied, in a bantering tone.

She smiled, in spite of her misgivings. His charmingly boyish enthusiasm was catching. 'Persuasion is something you're good at, Patrick. Of course I hadn't forgotten. But I was thinking about my work. I'll have to call in another trained nurse—we're terribly busy at the moment.'

'Call Jacqueline in reception—she'll fix it for you. Bring in as many nurses as you like, but make sure you're free this evening. I've booked seats at the Marigny theatre and a table at Maxim's afterwards.'

The corridor was deserted, and suddenly he pulled her close to him, kissing her gently on the lips.

'If only it were just the two of us,' she murmured, half under her breath.

'We must be patient,' he whispered. 'Soon. . .it will all be worthwhile.'

She pulled herself away as the sound of approaching footsteps echoed around the corner. They parted in opposite directions. Rebecca was quickly back into her work, arranging extra staff cover for her evening off and making sure that the obstetrics unit was running smoothly before she went off duty. Brigitte Taralon said she didn't mind missing New Year's Eve with her family. The extra money was vitally important to them.

Patrick had arranged that they should all meet in the bar at the Théâtre Marigny. Rebecca took the Métro to Franklin-Roosevelt station and emerged in the middle of the Champs-Elysées. The water from the illuminated fountains fell in spectacular arcs into the Rond Point. She paused for a moment to watch the beautiful, iridescent spray, creating sparkling rainbows before cascading into the waters of the pond. All around her she could hear the roar of the Paris traffic, but the Rond Point was an oasis of calm, a reminder that natural beauty could still survive in a busy city.

'I thought I might find you here.'

She turned at the sound of Patrick's voice, her pulses racing. 'I thought we were to meet in the theatre,' she said.

'I arrived early—I've been watching out for you. You won't let me down, will you, Rebecca?'

She hesitated. 'How might I let you down, Patrick?'

'By not playing your part. Remember to turn the charm on with Jacques. . .but not with me.'

She gave a deep sigh. 'I hope you know what you're doing, Patrick.'

'Trust me,' he said gently.

She turned away and gazed at the cascading fountains as she tried to remain calm. The words, 'trust me', were beginning to get on her nerves!

Patrick was looking across at the theatre. 'I think that's Jacques getting out of a taxi. I suggest you go and meet him, Rebecca. I'll wait here until I see Florence.'

Reluctantly she waited for the lights to change on the crossing. As the traffic on the Champs-Elysées hurtled to a halt she crossed, in time to see Jacques disappearing into the theatre.

She deposited her thick camel coat in the cloakroom, and went along to the little bar where she could see Jacques ordering a drink. Feeling completely out of character, she went up to him and gave him an effusive smile.

'Good evening, Jacques,' she said, trying to inject warmth into her voice. 'We seem to be the first to arrive.'

'Ah, *bonsoir*, Rebecca. How nice to see you again. What will you have? A glass of champagne, perhaps?'

She murmured her thanks as she accepted the glass. Jacques was busy ordering more champagne to be placed on ice for them to drink at the interval. She turned to watch the door, and her heart sank at the sight of Patrick and Florence walking in, arm in arm, looking genuinely happy to be together again.

Nervously she took a sip of her champagne. She wasn't going to enjoy this subterfuge one bit! She'd been dreading having to make up to Jacques, but she hadn't realised how the sight of Patrick and Florence together would affect her. It was weeks since she'd seen them like this.

As they came over to the bar, Florence looked radiant. The weak and weary expression had vanished completely. Rebecca remembered how she had envied this older, more sophisticated woman when she'd first arrived in Paris, that morning in the rue Ste-Catherine all those months ago. Florence had come out on to her balcony in a flowing robe and raised her perfectly manicured hand to wave goodbye to her children, who were in Patrick's car.

A wave of jealousy flooded through Rebecca. This was going to be one of the most difficult evenings of her life!

It was a classical play, *Phèdre* by Racine. In the half-light from their seats near the stage, Rebecca stole a glance at Florence and saw that she was obviously bored with the performance. She was much more interested in leaning against Patrick and occasionally whispering to him. And Patrick, far from seeming annoyed at Florence's infantile interruptions, positively encouraged her by smiling and leaning his head towards her.

Oh, the beast! Rebecca thought as she tried to concentrate on the play. Well, two could play at that game! Deliberately she dropped her programme on to the floor. She moved to pick it up, but Jacques, sitting beside her, was quicker than she.

'Allow me, my dear,' he said, placing the programme back on her lap.

The smile she bestowed on the charming French accountant came easily to her now that she was annoyed with Patrick! She turned to see if Patrick was watching, but his eyes were on the stage.

Pity he missed my performance, she thought. But it was getting easier to play the part Patrick had asked her to play.

They took a taxi to Maxim's when the final curtain came down. There had been many shouts of 'Bravo!' that delayed their departure considerably, but at last they had made it into the rue Royale and the taxi was drawing to a halt.

The maître d'hôtel greeted Patrick like a long-lost friend, then his eyes alighted on Florence. He expressed his delight at seeing the two of them together again.

Rebecca's spirits plummeted. Jacques had taken her arm as they left the taxi, and she leaned against him. The gesture was purely automatic, but he obviously took it as a sign of her interest, because he increased his attentions.

They had a round table, discreetly tucked away in a corner, with a white starched tablecloth and napkins, gleaming silver, tall candles and a central bouquet of roses. Rebecca chatted to Jacques throughout the meal and deliberately ignored Patrick and Florence, who seemed to be in a world of their own.

She watched Jacques's reaction to this, but he showed no interest in anyone but her. She glanced across at Florence and saw that she hadn't the slightest desire to attract Jacques's attention. The ploy simply wasn't working! As far as she could see, she was the only one who was feeling jealous!

But the food was superb, as she had expected in a prestigious restaurant like Maxim's. She started with *fricassée de sole et queues d'écrevisses*—crayfish mixed with sole; for her main course she chose *caneton au vinaigre de framboise*, which was a succulent duckling in a raspberry sauce. Patrick suggested they all finished with the *specialité de la maison, crêpes Veuve Joyeuse*.

Rebecca made a silent translation of this exquisite crêpes dessert. *Veuve Joyeuse* meant the Merry Widow. How apt! she thought as she watched the scintillating Florence, eyes shining with happiness.

Jacques suggested they all go back to his apartment for a nightcap. Rebecca opened her mouth to decline, but found herself outvoted.

It was after midnight. The new year had arrived as they sat at the table. As they went out into the cold, frosty first of January, the crowds were still milling around on the rue Royale. Jacques's apartment was not too far away, near the place Vendôme. He suggested it might be fun to walk as he took hold of Rebecca's arm and began to pilot her along.

He was a tall man, almost as tall as Patrick, and she found it anything but fun trying to keep up with his long strides. The cold night air was freezing her ears. She noticed that Florence, walking ahead with Patrick, was wearing a chic, snug little fur hat that matched her mink coat.

As she turned up the collar of her camel coat, Rebecca reflected that it wouldn't be long before she could escape this charade. She'd played the part better than she'd imagined would be possible, but now she was ready to be released. . .and longing to be alone with Patrick, if that was going to be possible.

She declined any more champagne at Jacques's apartment, but accepted coffee as she looked around at the typically masculine ambience of this elegant bachelor pad. It was obvious that Jacques had expensive tastes—and the money to go with it! He was a perfect match for Florence, so why didn't she take any notice of him?

At the same moment as this thought came to her, Jacques leaned across the sofa and whispered, 'Perhaps we could meet again, Rebecca?'

Oh, God, this is too much, she thought, putting her cup down on the side-table. There was a limit to how much she would go along with. She summoned up her idiot foreigner act again, pretending not to understand as she stood up, putting on a polite smile.

'What a delightful evening. I'm afraid I must go now—I'm on duty in a few hours. Got to get some sleep.'

She moved towards the door, expecting Patrick to follow her, but he remained at Florence's side.

'Please don't get up,' she told him. . .and he didn't! 'I'll take a taxi back to the apartment.'

'I'll call one for you,' said Jacques. 'Let me get your coat.'

She ducked out of Jacques's goodnight kiss by heading for the stairs instead of waiting by the lift with him. Turning to wave, she hurried away down the three flights that led out to the place Vendôme.

The polite smile she had worn most of the evening

evaporated as soon as she was alone. The taxi Jacques had ordered for her was waiting by the kerb. Curtly she gave the driver her address and sank back against the seat as the taxi sped across Paris back to the apartment block in the rue Ste-Catherine. As she closed the door of her *chambre de bonne*, she kicked off her shoes and padded across to the bed. Her clothes tumbled to the floor as she slipped, exhausted, between the sheets.

It seemed as if she had only been asleep for a few minutes when she heard the tapping at her door. She reached for her robe and padded across to peer through the spy-hole. Patrick's face was close to the door on the other side. For an instant she toyed with the idea of telling him to go away. The night out in a foursome had been a disaster as far as she was concerned. Everyone else seemed to have enjoyed it, but she didn't see why she should sacrifice her own pleasure because of Patrick's hare-brained scheme.

The tapping on the door continued. With a sigh of resignation she opened it.

'I'm sorry,' he said, taking her into his arms as soon as she'd closed the door. 'You didn't enjoy yourself, did you?'

'What an understatement!' Rebecca moved to pull herself away, but he was too strong for her. She glared up at him, suddenly aware of her crumpled appearance. Her hair must look a sight, and she'd been so tired she hadn't even bothered to remove her make-up. She wondered now if her mascara was smudged and decided it probably was.

'You played your part brilliantly!' he told her. 'Jacques adored you.'

'Patrick, if you remember, that wasn't the object of the exercise. We wanted Florence to adore Jacques. . .but you were so attentive to her that she didn't spare a glance at him.'

'Tactics, Rebecca,' he explained, bending down and dropping a kiss on her cheek.

This time she wrenched herself away. 'Your tactics aren't working, Patrick, and I've had enough. You've leaned over backwards to care for Florence. I'm beginning to think she's got some kind of hold over you. . .other than the fact that. . .'

Her voice trailed away as she saw the pained expression in his eyes.

'Other than the fact that my wife killed her husband,' he finished off tonelessly. 'Look, I can see you're very tired. I mustn't keep you talking when you have to be on duty in a few hours.'

He was moving away from her, his hand reaching for the door. She wanted to stop him leaving again, to hold on to him and explain that it was only her love for him that prevented her from sympathising with Florence. She felt he'd gone too far this time, but she still loved him.

But as he went out through the door she did nothing to stop him. And later, as she lay sleepless in her bed, she clutched at the gold chain around her neck and the tears began to fall.

She hadn't cried like this since she was a little girl— not since the day her father had walked out on them.

CHAPTER FIFTEEN

A WHOLE month passed, during which time Rebecca only saw Patrick occasionally, when their medical duties happened to coincide. Deep down inside, her feelings were numb; she knew she would have to do something to resolve the situation, but, as it transpired, the resolution was taken out of her hands.

Walking along the corridor one morning early in February, she was stopped by Sister Béatrice Dupond.

'I'm so sorry to hear the news, but you mustn't take it too badly,' the sister told her.

Rebecca stared at Béatrice Dupond. This time she didn't pretend she hadn't understood what her colleague had said. Although she had slept badly again, she was wide awake and intensely curious to know what Sister Dupond was talking about.

'You'd better enlighten me, because I've no idea. . .'

'Well, isn't that just typical?' Sister Dupond declared, with a triumphant smile. 'Dr Delan hasn't bothered to tell you yet. Well, Brigitte Taralon knows all about it.' She lowered her voice and whispered, 'If you ask me, he just wants to get rid of you because you know too much. There's a rumour going around that. . .'

Rebecca's pulses raced as she moved away quickly and made for the obstetrics unit. She didn't want any part of Sister Dupond's tittle-tattle. It would be some juicy piece of gossip about Florence, gleaned from Nurse Diane Poitiers.

Brigitte Taralon was sitting at her desk in the office. She looked up when Rebecca entered, but didn't move out of Rebecca's chair. 'Dr Delan asked if you would report to him as soon as you came in,' she said. 'He's asked me to take over your department. . .as from today.'

'He's what?' Rebecca felt as if she were part of a bad dream. Surely she would wake up any minute. She turned on her heel and ran down the corridor; she was too impatient to take the lift, and leapt down the stairs two at a time.

'Dr Delan is on the telephone,' Jacqueline, leaving Patrick's office after delivering the morning post, informed her.

'Is he, indeed?' Rebecca said through clenched teeth as she sailed into Patrick's office without knocking.

Patrick looked up and covered the mouthpiece with his hand. 'I'll be with you in a moment, Rebecca. If you——'

She stormed across the room, wrenched the phone from his hand and slammed it back on to its cradle. 'Now perhaps you'll tell me what's going on!'

His eyes blazed with anger as he came round the desk and stood towering above her. 'That was a very childish thing to do. I was speaking to an important client and——'

'And I'm not as important as a client, I suppose? I have to hear half-baked stories from the staff before you do me the courtesy of informing me!' She sank down into a chair so that her legs would stop trembling.

Patrick leaned back against the desk. The expression in his eyes had changed to one of concern.

'I'm sorry, I couldn't tell you anything until I'd checked with Brigitte Taralon. I had to be sure that she could take on a full-time appointment before I could have you transferred.'

The light was beginning to dawn. 'You're having me transferred. . .to La Colombière, I presume?'

'It will be excellent experience for you. . .and you'll see Chris again. I thought you'd like that.'

'You could have asked me first instead of taking this high-handed action. I love my work here in the obstetrics unit.'

'Thre's an excellent obstetrics unit at La Colombière . . .smaller, of course. . .and Sister Jeanne Manoir, the permanent sister, is due to take maternity leave. I've been trying to fill her place with someone suitable, and then I realised you would fit the bill admirably.'

Rebecca didn't believe this could be the man she had fallen in love with all those weeks ago. How could he treat her in this cavalier fashion? From deep inside her a little voice echoed the words of Béatrice Dupond: 'If you ask me, he just wants to get rid of you because you know too much.'

She stood up. There was nothing she could do to change things. If Patrick wanted her out of the way, it was best she went quickly. . .and with the minimum of fuss.

He put out his hand towards her, but she moved away, not trusting herself to speak.

He ignored her rejection. 'I would appreciate it,

Rebecca, if you could stay at La Colombière for the full three months of Sister's maternity leave. If that isn't possible I'll arrange for——'

'Don't worry, Patrick. I'll stay,' she told him.

She couldn't believe that events had happened so fast as she drove along the side of the Bois de Boulogne and headed for the Périphérique. Patrick had lent her one of the Clinique cars that did the run between La Colombière and Paris, being used by the medical personnel. She had studiously avoided saying goodbye, feeling that it would serve no purpose at all. She'd got her feelings under control now and she was resigned to the inevitable. All the feelings of misgiving and apprehension came flooding back now. She'd known all along it was too good to last. There had been too many obstacles in their path.

She took a hand from the wheel, fingering the gold chain around her neck. She had thought of handing it back, but that would have been too melodramatic. Far better to disappear from the Clinique unnoticed.

Her latest batch of mothers had been sorry to hear that she was going. Brigitte Taralon had said she would miss her, and Jacqueline had told her to hurry back. But she had told no one else. The grapevine could do that and the story of her swift departure would become intricately embroidered!

She reached La Colombière just as the sun was dipping down behind the coastal hills. It had never looked lovelier, with a thin sprinkling of snow on the ground and a hoar-frost on the branches of the trees.

The welcome from the staff was warm, especially

from Madame Thiret. Rebecca expressed her surprise that Chris wasn't there to meet her.

Madame Thiret gave her a conspiratorial smile. 'I expect he's in the swimming-pool with Karine.'

'Oh, you mean his physiotherapist? Are they getting on well?'

Madame Thiret nodded happily. 'What a stroke of luck for both of them! They're great friends.' She lowered her voice. 'Between you and me, Karine was something of a loner, unable to sustain a friendship, but she seems to have fallen for Chris. And what an improvement he's made! You won't recognise him. . .well, you know what a mess he was in; but he's all straightened out now. He's kicked the drugs habit and physically he's in excellent shape. There's no reason why he shouldn't be discharged, but Karine keeps insisting that he needs more treatment. I think we'll be hearing wedding bells before long.'

Rebecca's face gave her away; the surprise she felt was etched deep into her expression. Madame Thiret put out her hand and touched her arm.

'My dear, I know Chris used to be your fiancé. You're not still. . .?'

'Oh, good heavens, no!' Rebecca exclaimed, in a relieved tone. 'It was such a shock, that's all. I'm terribly happy for them.'

Later that evening Chris asked her almost the same question. As they sat together drinking coffee in the staff sitting-room after supper, Karine having left them discreetly alone, he quietly announced that he planned to see if Karine would go back to England with him.

'How would you feel about that?' he asked Rebecca.

She looked across at this young man she had loved once and felt nothing but relief. 'I should be delighted. . .and Chris, congratulations! You look terrific. You must have worked hard getting back into shape.'

'I had a good physiotherapist,' he said, with a wry grin. 'And love can work wonders. I'd rather thought you and Dr Delan would have——'

'We were just good friends, Chris,' she interposed quickly. 'Look, I must be off to settle myself into my new room.'

Chris smiled. 'Thanks for everything, Rebecca. If it hadn't been for you I'd never have met Karine. I'm going to ask her to marry me, now that I know how you feel.'

'And you can have my blessing,' Rebecca told him with a genuinely happy smile.

The weeks that passed were full of hard work for Rebecca. Professionally she was totally fulfilled, but deep down inside her emotions were like ice. She felt as she had done when she was a child, knowing that her father had gone and probably wouldn't be coming back. There was a constant feeling of rejection, and the only way she could cope was to build her own life and try to ignore her feelings. Life had to go on, and she was becoming very good at hiding her emotions. None of the staff had any idea how she felt. If anything, she over-compensated by being deliberately buoyant, enthusiastic and always ready to have some fun with her patients.

She came to regard her obstetrics unit at La Colombière with the same pride she'd had at the Clinique in Paris. And when, on a warm spring morning, she delivered a baby daughter to Jeanne Manoir, the permanent obstetrics sister, she knew that she would have to start considering her future. Her days at La Colombière were numbered, and she would have to come to a decision.

'Will you be going back to Paris when my maternity leave is over?' Jeanne Manoir asked, only hours after the delivery, as Rebecca went into her room.

Rebecca picked up the new baby from her crib at the side of her mother's bed and started to change her nappy.

'I'm not sure, Jeanne,' she said evasively. 'I'd like to stay on here. . .or I may go back to London. . .who knows?'

She flashed one of the brilliant smiles that she hoped fooled everyone into thinking she was happy. Well, she was content when she was on duty. It was only in the still small hours of the night that she felt despair gnawing away inside her, and longing, deep longing for what might have been if only. . .

'Your friend Chris went back to London, didn't he?' Jeanne's voice interrupted her thoughts. 'Do you miss him?'

Rebecca handed the baby over to its mother so that the breast-feed could begin. Then she sat down in a chair beside the bed.

'No, I don't miss him,' she replied truthfully. 'I'm glad Karine went with him, even if it did take a while to find a good replacement for her. I had a letter from them this week. They're both working in London and they plan to marry in the summer.'

'Ah, how lovely! I do like a happy ending, don't you, Rebecca?' said the young mother, her eyes shining as she looked down at her suckling infant.

For once, Rebecca found her acting talents had deserted her. There was a decidedly prickly sensation behind her eyes. She stood up, quickly, murmuring something about work to be done.

CHAPTER SIXTEEN

IT WAS almost Easter. The daffodils in the garden of La Colombière were in full bloom as Rebecca walked along the path that led to the edge of the cliff. Far below, she could see the beach where she had played as a child. It was her day off. Jeanne, the permanent obstetrics sister, had returned yesterday, having left her baby in the care of a willing granny. Nobody on the staff had quizzed Rebecca about what she was going to do, but it was obvious that the small obstetrics unit didn't require two sisters.

So, today, on her day off she had to come to a decision. She could take a junior post in the convalescent department, here at La Colombière; she could telephone the Paris Clinique and see what post they could offer her, or she could go back to London.

Decisions, decisions! She sat down on the ancient rustic seat that commanded a superb view of the bay, and tried desperately to organise her thoughts. She didn't want a junior position in the convalescent department. Quite frankly, it would bore her to tears after the excitement, unpredictability and responsibility of obstetrics. She had studiously avoided all contact with Paris during her three months in Brittany, but she had heard via the grapevine that Brigitte Taralon was an excellent sister and had no intention of leaving her obstetrics post. Rebecca decided she would be damned

182

if she'd go back to Paris and take on another position from scratch. Not while rumours were still circulating. . .as they surely must be.

She sighed. So it looked as if, by a process of elimination, she would go back to London.

There was a rustling sound in the tree high above her. A couple of doves were building a nest. '*Le colombier*, the dovecote,' she said softly to herself.

As she watched the happy pair she found herself wondering if they were descended from the original doves who had given their name to the family house that had been built here. Patrick's family's house. . .all those years ago, long before he was born. . .

The sound of tyres crunching on the gravel distracted her attention from the mating pair. She recognised the car, and her heart began to thump madly. Two men were getting out, both perfectly recognisable even from this distance. One was the accountant, Jacques Fromentin, and the other. . .

Oh, God! It was so long since she'd seen Patrick. She'd completely forgotten how he could throw her into a flat spin. She looked down at the old jeans she was wearing, the sloppy espadrilles and the crumpled cotton shirt that she'd pulled from the heap on her bedside chair. Florence wouldn't be seen dead looking as she did at the moment.

She started to get up, thinking that if only she could move carefully towards the cliff path she could escape the eyes of the two men.

'Rebecca!'

Too late! They were coming over. . .both of them.

Rebecca walked slowly towards them over the soft

dewy grass between the daffodils, one hand pushing her unruly auburn hair from her eyes.

'It's good to see you again, Rebecca,' Jacques greeted her, his voice warm and friendly.

'How are you?' asked Patrick, in the sort of voice he usually reserved for his patients.

She flashed him a brilliant but impersonal smile. 'Never better. . .and you?'

He returned her smile, and she tried to ignore the strong emotions that churned away inside her.

'I'm fine,' he said. 'But you must excuse me; I've got to tell Madame Thiret we've arrived.' He hesitated for a moment, his eyes deliberately averted. 'I believe Jacques would like a word with you.'

'Please don't let me detain you, Patrick,' she said, her heart sinking in spite of the tight rein she held on her emotions.

Patrick began to walk away towards the main house, and Rebecca turned to look at Jacques with a puzzled frown. 'How can I help you?'

He gave her a rueful grin. 'I think it's more I who can help you.'

Oh, no! He hadn't misinterpreted her again, had he? She took a deep breath. 'Look, Jacques, when we went out together in Paris you may have got the impression that. . .'

'Rebecca, I know all about the plan to make Florence jealous,' he interposed quickly.

She stared up at him. 'You do? How did you find out?'

'It was my idea in the first place. Patrick, being a

good friend of both Florence and myself, agreed to go
along with it.'

'But I don't understand. Are you telling me that. . .'

He took hold of her arm. 'Let me explain, but first I
think you should sit down.'

She offered no resistance as he led her back to the
seat at the edge of the cliff.

'Florence and I go back a long way. We were lovers
before she met Michel. When Florence was still in her
teens, we had a silly quarrel; Florence had become
jealous. I married the girl Florence was jealous of and
eventually she met Michel. Years later, when both our
partners had died, we met again. One night, when you
were out with Patrick, I believe, she invited me round
for a late supper in the kitchen. She'd sent the maid to
bed and made me a special dessert of——'

'So it was you the maid heard in the kitchen that
night,' Rebecca interrupted.

Jacques sighed. 'I'm afraid so. And it was because of
me that Florence tried to commit suicide. She wanted
us to marry, but I said it was too soon and. . .look,
you know what happened after that. I don't need to
tell you any more. I can see you believe me, don't you,
Rebecca?'

She drew in her breath. 'I'm stunned by what you've
told me, but of course I believe you, Jacques. Why do
you ask?'

He didn't answer her at first, and she saw that he
was waving to someone on the outside balcony of the
house. She looked up and saw Patrick wave back
before disappearing into an upstairs room.

'Patrick's coming down to answer all your questions.

He wanted to make sure you believed me. You had been so sceptical of what he'd told you before.'

'And with good reason!' she flung at him. 'Oh, it's no good me taking it out on you, Jacques. You may have been the one who thought up the devious plan to get Florence jealous, but Patrick was the one who carried it out. And as far as I could see he was enjoying every minute. There was absolutely no chance that it would work. Florence is only interested in Patrick, and Patrick is only. . .'

She stopped in mid-sentence as Patrick sprinted across the lawn to stand in front of her, his eyes blazing angrily.

'That's where you're wrong, Rebecca. The plan worked. Florence telephoned Jacques the very next day after we'd all been out together, to ask him if he was serious about you. He invited her out, and one thing led to another as we hoped it would. They're getting married next week.'

Rebecca stared up at Patrick. 'I don't believe it!'

'It's true, Rebecca,' Jacques put in. 'And now I'm going to leave you two together. You've got a lot of catching up to do.'

From up above them, the doves began to bill and coo as if in a chorus of approval as Patrick leaned across the seat and pulled Rebecca into his arms. She wanted to resist; she wanted to show him that he couldn't drop her and pick her up again at a moment's notice. She tensed her body, summoned up all her strength to quell the conflicting emotions, but in the end she succumbed to the delicious primeval feeling that was floating over her.

And as her dormant sensuality returned in the middle of a long, lingering kiss, she wondered, inconsequentially, if this was where Patrick's predecessors had sat when they wanted a romantic interlude.

Several blissful minutes later she pulled away, the sound of the waves crashing on the shore far below bringing her back to her senses.

'I suppose you think I've forgiven you, Patrick Delan,' she said, in a pseudo-solemn voice. 'But I haven't. There was no need to send me away like that.'

He cupped her chin with his hands and looked deep into her eyes with a meltingly tender expression. 'Oh, but there was. I couldn't bear to have you around while Florence and Jacques's romance was in the balance. I knew it was touch and go, and if they split up again I would be left to pick up the pieces. And there were strange rumours flying about the Clinique intimating that I'd been instrumental in Florence's attempted suicide. I didn't want you to hear them.'

She remained silent. There was no need for Patrick to know that even she had doubted him.

'But why did you cover up for Jacques?' she asked.

'It was a question of loyalty to an old friend,' he explained. 'Jacques's family and mine have always been close. His family helped with the financial arrangements when the nursing home was opened at La Colombière. Jacques is brilliant in financial matters, but hopeless at everything else. I knew if he was quizzed about Florence's accident he'd go to pieces.'

'So you decided to ride out the storm by yourself, taking all the blame if necessary,' she said softly, looking up into the deep blue eyes of the man she loved so much and feeling her heart wanting to burst with pride.

'I did what had to be done,' he corrected. 'It was a medical matter and I knew I could handle it better than Jacques. I knew that he was sorry he'd told Florence he didn't want to marry. He told me he was simply playing for time; he didn't feel ready to commit himself after several years of being a bachelor. But he had no idea she would take an overdose. He begged me to help him convince Florence that he loved her and wanted to marry her.'

'So that was when the pair of you cooked up that hare-brained scheme,' Rebecca commented drily.

His eyes danced mischievously. 'It couldn't have been all that hare-brained. . .it worked, remember? I told you at the time that your performance was brilliant.'

She gave him a wry grin. 'Perhaps I should change my profession and become an actress. What do you think?'

'How about becoming my wife instead?'

'I'm afraid I'll have to think about that one.'

Patrick pulled her closer. 'How long will it take you to give me an answer? Jacques is staying on here for a few days, but I've got to be back in Paris tomorrow, and I'd like to take you with me.'

'I could be persuaded. . .'

'I'll persuade you on the way back. I thought we could spend the night at the Lion d'Or again. *Madame* wouldn't be shocked if I ordered a double room this time. Not if we announce our engagement. . .'

4 MEDICAL ROMANCES
AND 2 FREE GIFTS
From Mills & Boon

Capture all the excitement, intrigue and emotion of the busy medical world by accepting four FREE Medical Romances, plus a FREE cuddly teddy and special mystery gift. Then if you choose, go on to enjoy 4 more exciting Medical Romances every month! Send the coupon below at once to:

**MILLS & BOON READER SERVICE, FREEPOST
PO BOX 236, CROYDON, SURREY CR9 9EL.**

NO STAMP REQUIRED

 ✂ ----------------------------------- ✂

YES! Please rush me my 4 Free Medical Romances and 2 Free Gifts! Please also reserve me a Reader Service Subscription. If I decide to subscribe, I can look forward to receiving 4 Medical Romances every month for just £6.40, delivered direct to my door. Post and packing is free, and there's a free Mills & Boon Newsletter. If I choose not to subscribe I shall write to you within 10 days - I can keep the books and gifts whatever I decide. I can cancel or suspend my subscription at any time. I am over 18.

EP19D

Name (Mr/Mrs/Ms) ——————————————————

Address ————————————————————————

————————————————————————————

———————————————— Postcode ——————

Signature ——————————————————————

mps
MAILING
PREFERENCE
SERVICE

— MEDICAL ♥ ROMANCE —

The books for enjoyment this month are:

SAVING DR GREGORY Caroline Anderson
FOR LOVE'S SAKE ONLY Margaret Barker
THE WRONG DIAGNOSIS Drusilla Douglas
ENCOUNTER WITH A SURGEON Janet Ferguson

♥   ♥   ♥   ♥   ♥

Treats in store!

Watch next month for the following absorbing stories:

THE SINGAPORE AFFAIR Kathleen Farrell
CAROLINE'S CONQUEST Hazel Fisher
A PLACE OF REFUGE Margaret Holt
THAT SPECIAL JOY Betty Beaty